N O T
T H E
HERO:

IT WAS ALWAYS FOR SUNDAY

a   rashaun   smith   project

Love 4 Bullets Publishing

A
RaShaun Smith
Project

Not the Hero: It Was All for Sunday
© 2017, RaShaun Smith
All rights reserved

Editors: Lisa Cerasoli and Adrian Muraro
www.529books.com

Cover Design: RaShaun Smith
Interior Design: Matt Dimond
www.matthewdimond.com

This is for you, mom and dad. This is for every Lego you had to step on in the dark, every time I wasn't home before the streetlights came on, and every phone call I avoided in search of my daily fix for solitude. This is for loving me so completely I felt comfortable enough to get constantly lost in my own world.

One day I'll mourn the fact neither one of you got to read this, but that is not today. Thank you, Betty and Warren. And if per chance I get to choose my parents in the next life I will choose you again.

PROLOGUE
WE ARE NOT THEM

New Mexico, 2007

"Where the fuck did he go?" I said, banging on the roof of the beater we stole just a minute ago.

We were in New Mexico—some shit town with clay structures everywhere—on the errant promise of finding the end to this fucking misery.

"He must've survived that crash," Drake answered, squinting to survey the scene under the duress of direct sunlight. The summer sun is brutal in New Mexico.

"Damn! He didn't look like he could pull it off that fast," I responded.

"He has remained under everyone's radar this entire time."

"Still...."

"Fuck, I'm even surprised there was a fucking reading at all," Drake continued, half-amused.

The scene was gruesome. At possibly the busiest crossroad any town in this state possessed was a nine-car pileup. Nothing but twisted metal frames and mangled limbs. The target, RagnokForce, must've lost control of his car and went directly into an innocent SUV trying to turn before the light went red. Glass shards illuminated the scene like a winter pageant.

"Well, let's take a look," Drake ventured.

Drake met me in the front of the car as we moved toward the wreckage. Dust from the sand-drowned road settled around our feet in little clouds with each step.

The unforgiving heat was as tangible as the ground beneath us. Such a consistently high temperature bred acceptance to uncontrollable and unforeseen death—the type of malaise that makes you barely raise an eyebrow to random death, even if it involves loved ones. No wonder the gathering crowd took to us with uncommon curiosity, reverence, and complete lack of fear.

"Hey, when did you lose part of your tooth?" Drake asked me suddenly.

My mind raced back to a sticky moment where I was left to battle Hosts while Drake was nowhere to be found. Activeskin protects one from all things mortal, but can't shield the impact of a punch from a giant.

"You don't remember me taking on seven or eight Hosts back in Idaho?" I asked, doing my best to keep my anger and deny the urge to form a small dagger with one of my battlebraces, then launch it directly into his side just for spite.

"Naw, not really," Drake replied, nonchalant.

"Yeah, cause you were just taking your sweet fucking time strolling and whistling toward my position."

"He got that fucker good," Drake continued, angling his neck left and right to get a better view at the gaping hole in my right molar. "Looks like the whole crown was knocked off."

As we got closer, we could see the bodies from the crash lying halfway out of the destroyed vehicles. We strolled up to survey the scene. Mangled bodies and shattered glass did not explain the missing signal on the navguide, unless our quarry was killed by impact. I could hear people asking us questions...I just didn't care.

"Anything over there?" I yelled to Drake, who was now standing on the other side of the massive wreck.

"Nada. This fucker must've been obliterated."

"Obliterated?"

"Obliterated."

"You don't really believe that, do you?"

"I don't know, Salt. I don't care."

"So, let's review," I said, coming around to join Drake. "We had him."

"We did," he confirmed.

"Got in a shootout about a mile back," I said, pointing in the opposite direction.

"We fired," Drake added.

"Think you managed to erase a whole city block."

"I think this entire town is the equivalent of a city block, but whatever."

"Right. He gets into a car and speeds off."

"We chase," Drake said.

"He gets into a car accident that would kill any normal and at least wound a hero, and now he's gone."

"What do you want me to tell you? Wouldn't be the first time, Salt. It doesn't matter. It's fucking miserable out here. It might be 130 degrees. Can we at least waste time discussing your need to investigate every funky element to our miserable charge in life in somewhere slightly cooler than the devil's balls?"

"Does it not bother you that—"

"No! It doesn't. Whatever you were going to say it doesn't. What does is that I'm fucking hot. AC, now!"

"Where?"

"I don't know. Maybe that strip club around the corner?"

The location of titty bars never ceases to amaze me. You would think they'd be reserved to the seediest nether regions of a downtown area. That only in the shadows of your proper establishments does the glow from the requisite neon-lit LIVE NUDE GIRLS, and/or any combination of the three, appear. But then, without notice, while admiring the late eighteenth-century Mexican-influenced architecture of the La Iglesias de Cristo, Victoria's Cabaret is reminding you that they too have religion and two-for-one lap dances. And the Dirty Venus just down the street has the most pretty nude girls this side of the Rio Grande. Amazing.

Considering we had little-to-no answers facing us, a little T&A-themed leisure time sounded like the best idea going.

Once we got inside, I went right for the bathroom. Drake didn't mind. His eyes were set on a prime location right up front of the stage. The bathroom was remarkably small for a strip club, almost personal. Looking down at the sink, I saw a toothbrush and toothpaste. Before the Battles, you'd have to pay me in the six figures to do what I was about to. But before the Battles, I also didn't cross the country hunting people like me.

C H . 1
MINTY FRESH TRUTH

Sunday was waiting for me in the dirty little bathroom. She looked both annoyed and pleased, like she killed her target, but had to work much harder than she had planned. It's that aspect of her that scared me more than her penchant to show up from the unknown.

"I swear to Christ, I'm fucking done with bars," I said, choosing to ignore her and reach for toothbrush.

"You're not really going to do that, are you?" she asked, eyeing the random person's tooth-cleaning items I was preparing to use.

"Gross, sure, but the cool, minty taste of toothpaste has almost become foreign to me. When it was a simple, necessary, everyday annoyance, I just didn't recognize the value it truly held. The feat it accomplishes—making it at least tolerable to speak to one another in face-to-face situations—is not small in the grand scheme of things. Suffice to say, the world needs toothpaste. And so do I."

"Why the lovely ode that has you brushing your teeth with a toothbrush that probably contains a new form of hepatitis?"

"I got cavities, my friend. I got a bum tooth that has a hole the size of a pea going straight to the root of my gum. I got enough tarter to build a high-rise building's foundation with."

Sunday crossed her arms. "I'm not your friend."

"Then why are you here?"

"He sent you here to kill the last Recluse. Don't do it."

"I'm too tired to play coy, so let's just say you are talking about Samytus."

"Of course I'm talking about him. He wants Drake to kill the hero he sent you here for. Don't do it."

I focused on my reflection in the mirror, rather than on the action of jamming a toothbrush I found in a strip club bathroom into my mouth or Sunday's ominous words. She continued to talk, but I trailed away.

My mind wandered into our lives these days, and toothpaste. Goddamn, did I love toothpaste these days. But also, how did she know about what Samytus wanted? Why did she care? How did she always know where to find me?

Chaos erupted outside. I could hear Drake doing his best to calm down a bouncer. Not sure what the problem was, but the bouncer seemed adamant that he wasn't fond of repeating himself.

I ignored it. I needed time to think, without everything moving around us. None of us asked to be their subjects, to become heroes, but at least there was a promise to an end. After the heroes we'd killed, after seeing what they could do before we managed to take them down, I wasn't so sure an end was possible. I was no longer sure an end was ever intended. My best bet was to kill as many of the Employers as I could.

Even the slap from Sunday couldn't bring me back to the present. I was lost in my thoughts and memories of how I got to this point. I barely heard her say, "Listen to me, you lost fuck, because for the past year, I've been saving your life."

C H . 2
BOWL #2 & THE
BEGINNING TO AN END

The Beginning of the Battles. Boston, MA, 2006

Church is now in session, I thought as I lay myself back down onto the floor, accepting the impending comatose state. Happiness crept over me like a filthy lover I should despise, but can't pull myself away from.

Incredible—for a brief second, I was back in that skeezy period of time in my misbegotten youth where techno clubs and $4.50 bottled water were cool.

The TV blared some irrelevant rants and rationalizations from a sports panel show fielded by narcissistic sports journalists. It was hilarious to me how expert opinions on professional sports can be formed by simply writing about it for a period of time, or from experiences in their last year of playing sports—most likely right before they said hello to high school.

Today looked to be as unproductive as the last. A sly grin slinked from ear to ear from the immense, distracting amusement I gained from watching the thick, opaque, dark greenish-gray smoke escape my lungs and fill the room. Like tiny clouds musing about their own atmosphere; a world onto itself, stuck inside my decrepit old apartment. Everything else—my dwindling bank account, my lack of employment prospects, my penchant for not caring, all slowly faded away along with the little grayish-green clouds.

It's amazing how time halts to a standstill when you are among the unemployed but woefully housed. My roommates longed for the day I wasn't there. But for now, I was beyond content with my fear and loathing in Boston. Forgive me, Mr. Del Toro.

This was what my days were like since moving back from Alabama. Get up every afternoon to the mating call of lawn care equipment, working diligently outside. Go to the gym. Smoke weed. Get something to eat. Apply for jobs online. Play video-games, especially Circle Prophesy. Watch TV. Eat. Play more vid-eogames, but mostly Circle Prophesy. A little naughty time thanks to internet porn. Find my bed before dawn announces a new day. Close my eyes for a restful, worry-free slumber. The next day, rise fully rested and ready to repeat.

My days were so alike one another, my ability to gauge what day of the week it actually was rested solely on whichever two I was scheduled to work at the dive bar down the street—my proud, sole source of income…all $200 a week of it.

In all aspects that measure of a young college grad, I was non-existent. A waste, I mentally jested while creating mountains of debt, venturing further into satisfaction with making just enough to pay rent and a bill a month. I felt neither ambition nor the sense of urgency one should harbor when "one bill a month" is one out of twelve. But a year of sampling what was willing to hire me created a motivational lull more profound than any THC could develop—though the weed helped. Complacency was comfortable.

You would think that after being an independent agent of National Ground Postal Service, a commercial check-clearing processor, and a "model" talent agent, I would set my sights higher than trying to frag some punk kid or some old guy living in his mom's basement—a plausible future for me at this point—online. But I didn't.

I guess I grew into apathy by the prospects life had to offer at the moment. I dreaded my mother's daily phone check-ins, to the point that I was ecstatic when my phone got cut off every once in a while. When it wasn't cut off, I mostly avoid it out of shame.

The talks were repetitive, supportive, and firm. It was odd how similar her speeches were to one of my sales manger's pep talks. Both would mostly boil down to the fact that I should be doing better, purely on the fact that I graduated college. Or to quote the sales manager, "a fucking college graduate." Uplifting.

I knew neither of my parents could understand their son. I was nothing like my sister. Even though I am the youngest, my parents had to tighten their grip on me, because she was the perfect child. I guess I always wanted to escape. Just never could figure out to where, or why.

C H . 3
CHAOS RULES

The house shuddered as strangers rushed in. Their images blurred in my eyes, hazy with THC. The men were colossal, all in the upper-six-foot range, with physiques that were long and muscular. They boasted bald scalps and vacant, black eyes.

A silly grin returned to my face; my comically big new audience amused me. There were seven, by my count. My thoughts worked in idiosyncratic succession. Why was the "major" earthquake that had haunted every newsroom of every greater New England news station set aside for plausible urban legends happening? What drug did I miss taking that my sudden growth in company was at all plausible?

They were eerily silent, observing my erratic movements as I tried my best to stand and greet my surely fictitious mates. Though fathoms beyond shocked, I couldn't help but laugh at any reason for having extremely large random men in my house. I was seeing my own anti-drug commercial play out.

So far, these were the best reasons I could conjure up as to why these men were in my presence:

· It was time for my complementary alien anal probe, Weekly World News-style.

· A friend had gone above and beyond for the record books with a well-devised, and might I say, flawlessly executed, joke.

(Or if you will, prank.)

· Perhaps a new high I achieved from weed holds hallucinogenic potential?

· Or I'm dreaming one tripped-out dream, and just forgot that I passed out. Passing out has a funny way of doing that.

All, I suppose, were entirely possible. But all were also completely absurd.

From early childhood, I've been plagued by a picturesque imagination. It has led to sleepless nights after horror movies, to an Othellan social life cursed with seeds of deceit planted by the jealous and ill-willed surrounding me—resulting ultimately in breakups with girlfriends. Even when it was obvious that my imagination or dreams were just plain wrong, they held no less power over my conscious self.

Suddenly, one of my figments reached out and grabbed my right arm. Absolutely ridiculous, I thought. The pressure around my bicep felt almost identical to someone actually grabbing me. Nope. I stood corrected. It was identical to the pressure of being grabbed. You could even argue I was being pulled toward the hallway by this imaginary and super strong arm attached to a fictitious, huge, bald dick.

I continued to laugh as I was being pulled. Contemplating the validity of this moment was more pressing than trying to escape. The strange men showed no reaction to my sudden outburst—apart from closing in on all sides, that is.

Opening my eyes after fits of more laughter, the fictitious men's breath hit me from all sides. This gave reason to sober up and observe my surroundings with more effort. Foolish and active imaginations don't move hairs on your arm and neck.

I began to pray it was the weed, and that it only meant I needed to get more of that shit.

Without any notice, the six remaining strangers crept ever closer and grabbed any available space on my person. The pressure was no longer deniable; my consciousness had just reached the region of my brain that distinguished between laughable fantasy and disconcerting reality, confirming that it was now time to be concerned. In the moment, the best I could come up with was that someone ratted me out as some high-ranking drug dealer, and the DEA sent a team bordering on Hitler's pornographic vision of the ubermench after me.

But that made almost as much sense as their sudden appearance. I couldn't remember being rich enough to by more than a quarter at a time, and had only sold here and there—if one can call charging friends you don't really like a little more for a bag you bought from someone else "selling." Even if someone did sell me out to buy some freedom, the DEA had to be a little more sophisticated than to go hard and wet into the first address given to them by some perp saving his or her own ass. There had to be some surveillance suggesting there was no activity here at all. Shit, they probably knew how much weed I had better than I did.

Now, that reason thrown out, I moved to the next assumption—which, naturally, meant that I was the target of the biggest, most well-dressed hate group I'd ever heard of. A bit much for just one 5'9" black man, though. No, the Klan is too pussy and too dumb to dress this well for a good ole lynching. And Arians... well, the same can be said for them, too, but with more violent vernacular.

So with those entirely plausible reasons thrown out, the next assumption was that this was a joke. The type of joke where either my grandkids will tell their grandkids about, or the kind where something goes horribly wrong and a lot of blood from a lot of people winds up in a lot of odd places. Yeah, dumb. No one in my social circle was going to those lengths for my mere humiliation.

I didn't have time to mentally investigate any other reason, because the men began to pull me harder toward the door leading downstairs. They were probably expecting a simple extraction, and a minute before they came, it was all I could feasibly hope for. But hope can be synonymous with assumption, and that rarely ends as intended.

I didn't feel my arm wrench back from the grips of two uninvited guests. I wasn't entirely aware of my right shoulder slipping seamlessly from the grasp of the strangers behind me. And when my left arm shot forward into the chest of the one directly in front of me at an unfamiliar speed, I couldn't help but to be more amazed with the sudden release of awesome power and how it felt than where it came from. A frightening realization of previously unknown power tingled down to my fingertips.

All I could do was stagger back, along with the strangers around me. We were all in astonishment of this force and pain I just created. They continued to step back in anticipation.

I smiled.

With the immediate area around me clear—and for a reason I wasn't sure of—I was about to bring some shit.

The waiting ended. The man I punched rushed forward, only to be met with a flurry of fists, connecting precisely with his chest and head. The stranger behind me seized my shoulders again, while another closed in to help subdue me.

A foreign instinct controlled my every move. I twisted my body as it rose, planting my left foot into the incoming stranger's chest as my right climbed to connect with his head.

Now facing the assailant behind me, I calmly blocked his attacks while stepping back. My newfound fighter's instinct guided me gracefully beneath another attack and closer to the next that rose to the challenge. I grabbed hold of the highest point I could reach on his body and jumped up, driving the crown of my skull into his chin, then pushing off him with my feet. A loud, hollow crack rang through the air.

Massive bodies and apartment walls were crumbling before me. The entryway of my living room was nearly two feet wider. Yet somehow, I was still standing—and, strangely, wanting more.

Those that weren't broken and withering on the ground tried in earnest to capture their disobedient quarry. Even with the small series of victories I was now conscious of, I couldn't shake the feeling that these guys were holding back. Escape had to become my next action.

Ducking the haymaker of one I left with a shattered jaw, I slipped into my bedroom, across from the living room. Without thinking, I burst through my window with only my arms crossed over my face for protection, landing cleanly on the grassy hill that lined the house. Glass and fragments of wood from my shattered window showered down behind me, outlining my body.

The canals of my brain raced with thousands of questions, and all demanding answers. Who were those men? Why were they after me? Why wasn't I more frightened?

I couldn't understand how I instantly knew how to take out three seven-foot men in a hallway my roommates and I struggled to get a couch through. Jumping through a glass window only to land like the Terminator was just scary. Either I was dead, or I should've been.

I took off down the street, hoping to lose them in open ground before they could follow me out. I cursed myself for not grabbing the car keys, but then remembered my car would only be useful in Raynham, where it was impounded. My roommates had yet to apologize for getting so many parking tickets.

The air was rare, cold crispness awarded selectively in the New England summers. Every star was visible. The night sky looked as real as it had ever looked to me; I almost felt like I was seeing it for the first time.

Running downhill would be obvious, so I chose to run uphill instead, to the intersection of Washington and Market Street. The right street had to bear many witnesses. If my mind had finally snapped from habitual drug abuse, the public will be quick to point that out.

Funny enough, there wasn't a car or person to be found. Even funnier was the absence of any sound associated with a residential area—no traffic in the distance, no dogs barking in backyards, no people bustling about, no crickets chirping. These details brought me out of my hard stride to look around.

I was beginning to feel as if I'd unknowingly slipped into some movie set that was clandestinely filming in my neighborhood and had just closed down for the night. Vacant houses with vacant windows glowed vacant stares back at me, whispering through the wind that there was no life to be found here.

"Hellokilla!"

I turned to trace the yell. The voice belonged to a man standing in the middle of the intersection. He was about my height, but bald like those other guys. His indistinct black suit fit perfectly around his medium frame. He smirked his face into hellish fleer.

"Resume test," he said, apparently to himself.

In the next instant, 400 strangers identical to the ones I'd left bloodied and dazed in my destroyed living room encircled me. They inched closer with every passing second.

You'll need one more, was all I could think as I clenched my fists and smiled back.

C H . 4
SPEAK AS
FRIENDS WOULD

I woke in a cell. A deep, pulsating, white-glowing cubed cell with nothing on the walls, nothing on the ceiling or floors, and nothing in the room except for me. There were no doors. There were no lines in the walls to suggest a separation or an opening.

I began to question if I was even in a cube at all, for the angles diminished into the abyss of pure pulsating white. I questioned if I were sitting, considering I had nothing to sit on.

I'm alone was my only thought. I had faint thoughts of another life, but nothing more substantial to take my mind away from the feeling of being utterly and unquestionably alone. My head screamed at me in anger and confusion for something else to think about, something else to focus on. But my mind's defense mechanisms—in this case, an internal scream—proved as powerful as a water pistol against a brush fire.

Even with my brain screaming in silent agony, my body felt relaxed. I was protesting something, but the rest of my being felt glad to be in my happy, white, glowing cell. I wasn't captive. I wasn't inclined to run.

My cell had a beat. A series of beats. More like a trance. I couldn't hear it at first. My thoughts were too loud, too many, too strong. There were so many questions running mad in my head. I couldn't stop asking where I was, or why didn't I care. The two conflicting ideas battled each other something fierce in my blank, aching head.

Once I noticed it, I could feel it. I could feel it tracing over my body with faint sensations, similar to standing too close to neon lights. Then it was communicating with me. A hum, a hiss, then random words turned into phrases, into sentences, until, shortly after, we were vaulted into continuation of an epic conversation. We spoke to one another as old friends. It felt good. Oh, I've missed you, I thought.

"This isn't yours." A sultry female voice whispered to me from within my being.

I couldn't escape the feeling that all else ceased to exist when I felt the communication between her and me. Felt—I didn't hear a thing coming from the cell, yet I heard her clearer than anything I had ever heard in my life. So clear that when the voice wasn't talking, it left a cold absence within me.

Even though I only consciously began to hear her, the conversation felt like it had been going on for some time. I wasn't scared of her. Nor was I comfortable, but I felt a need to engage. An obligation, really. But I hadn't a clue how. I just waited, believing that I would hear her again.

"Tonight is more true than those before," the voice continued.

The room seemed linked to the voice. Each syllable, each nuance and hesitation made the cell pulsate. Was I even in a room, or a dream manifesting a quasi-attempt at communicating with my consciousness? Was I even alive?

"Find whose hero you will become. Happy hunting."

C H . 5
AT THE VERY LEAST, A WELL-ORGANIZED GROUP OF JUNKIES

It was quite a sight to behold, the majesty of sunlight smacking the golden dome of Boston's Statehouse. One can forget how beautiful she is as she rests atop the Common and smiles down on all her subjects. I had spent many summers ignoring that image. I'm afraid that lost time won't be replaced by promises to see it again.

My head was still pounding, but worse now, as if something had been removed. It throbbed from side to side, front to back. I felt cold, but from within. An odd feeling in the dead days of a Boston summer, where the humidity alone could broil the senses to senselessness and drive the most docile to homicidal.

I couldn't recall travelling to the Common. Last thing I remembered, I was lounging in my humble abode, enjoying some of Dorchester's finest piff—or as the elders call it, grass. I certainly didn't recall participating in some art class among a bunch of randoms all standing as I was—lobotomized, vacant, staring ahead at some man presenting instructional material with the use of a plain flipchart.

The presenter was slightly on the diminutive side. He stood a shade over 5'6", with a bald white head that reflected the midday sun like a piss-ant third grader who just learned how to refract sunlight into someone's face with his Timex. Though plain enough in body and facial features, he gave off a brooding demeanor, with eyes hidden behind dark shades and a sharp, tailored suit that clung to him like faded body paint. If that wasn't enough, the smug grin hanging on his face even as he spoke only promised hell.

He held a simple baton to point to the objects of discussion on his simple flipchart. His 7'2" clone, dressed exactly as he was, stood by his side and diligently flipped the sheets, right on time with no obvious cues.

After a moment or so, the throbbing subsided. I hadn't noticed it before, but when it was throbbing so hard and so consistently, I couldn't hear anything else. Guess I simply didn't care about it in the face of the crippling pain.

As it is with coming into the middle of any conversation, I was confused at first. But slowly, I began to understand what he was saying. Apparently, I was the only one out of sync, as everyone else nodded in unison from time to time.

I shouldn't have been surprised that no one around us had noticed a random class taking place in the Common, at the foot of the Statehouse. Boston denizens are remarkably immune to the oddities that take place within the gates of the Common. To them, we were suckers either taking part in a scam, a tour, or both.

The smaller of the bald suits up front was currently talking about the image on the flipchart. It was an illustration of a man's silhouette, a simple black drawing with an even simpler, thick, light-blue line traced around it. The word "activeskin" was written above it.

C H . 6
Unaccustome
to   Unusal
Interactions

The impromptu seminar in the Common ended shortly after I became conscious of my new surroundings. It didn't feel like we covered much. It felt more like we were just a poor, disillusioned group of well-dressed and well-fed junkies, watching another junkie and his huge cohort explain nonsense with visual aids prepared by some fifth grade art class. There were pictures of guns and men leaping off buildings. The bald guy pointed to drawings of a GPS-like bracelet and spoke at length on how this was not a map to follow, but more of a radar of our surroundings.

He then proceeded to explain, in very rudimentary terms, two bracelets (one being the said GPS-like bracelet) and how they were supposed to be some violent extension of our imagination. I think at that point, I was more amused by the actual junkies beginning to join us with curiosity and bewilderment, as if they were supposed to be there and just forgot.

However, curiously enough, the presenter ended by expressing that all this wouldn't end until there was just one left. He illustrated this point with a flipchart page depicting a simple cartoon of two halves. One half had a group, with "start" written over it. The other half had one person, with "end" written over it.

Now with the class over, people wandered off in their own directions. It wasn't clear if we were given a direction to follow. People just walked silently, with their heads tucked. Some were crying; some were simply shaking their heads, as if they were doing their best to forget the last few hours. Maybe they thought they were dreaming. None of this felt like a dream to me, despite the fact that I didn't remember leaving my house and hopping the MBTA bus to the Red Line, then to the Downtown Crossing stop to go to the Common.

One of the junkies made eye contact with me and began to make his way through the crowd. He was determined but polite in his aggressive navigating, sometimes even pausing to allow a group of crying people to pass in peace.

I can't say I'm accustomed to being approached by the homeless, but I don't look to avoid the situation when it occurs. I get a weird insight from them. There's logic in their lost journeys in lives turned toward seemingly self-induced madness. As far as I'm concerned, we are all a little mad in the head. If you spend enough time in the city, you'll come to understand all her children. The real questions, however, were why now, and why was he approaching me in such haste?

A shapeless man halted the homeless gentleman before he could make his way to me. The newcomer clutched a notebook like a missionary clutches a bible as he pleaded with the homeless junkie. They looked like they were in a one-way argument, where the junkie continued to shake off the words of the stout man until finally, the junkie walked off with the stout man in reluctant tow.

C H . 7
SOME PEOPLE
JUST DON'T PAY
ATTENTION...

"You got a light?" the junkie asked. A tightly-wrapped, almost professional-looking blunt was hanging out of his mouth.

"That depends...you going to share?" I asked, nodding to his blunt.

He took it out and looked it over a moment, then placed it back into his mouth. "Yeah. I think it's big enough."

"Will you tell him, please?" the portly little man asked, exasperated.

"Shut it, fatty," the junkie hushed. His hands were clenched, but remained by his side.

"Umm, sorry, buddy. Don't have one," I responded after doing an honest search for a lighter in my pockets.

"No matter," he said calmly. "May I see your left forearm?"

The question made me want to look down. What haven't I noticed yet? Before I could go into another self-induced coma from all my internal questioning, he reached down and yanked my left forearm up and into view, with little concern for my shock.

The hairs on the back of my neck shot up. Part of the reason was because some random junkie had just grabbed my arm; the other was my forearm—both forearms.

There, discretely wrapped in spindly clear casings of sheer, gel-like plastic were the very same braces the bald man was educating us on with flipcharts earlier. I wish I had paid more attention.

There was a slight opening about an inch long toward the bottom of both braces, near the wrists. The one on my left forearm, which captured my new friend's attention, had a screen displaying a myriad of data moving at insane speeds.

"Some people just don't pay attention," the little fat man behind the junkie snorted in disgust.

"According to fat boy, we are teammates," the junkie said, pointing at a green dot on the screen.

It glowed at a pace similar to my white cube in the dream I had before randomly showing up in the Common.

"They're surprisingly lightweight, aren't they?" he continued.

"What's going on? What is all this, and who the fuck are you two?" I asked.

"These are called battlebraces," the little fat man answered excitedly. "Or at least, that is what our Host called them. I like to refer to them as gauntlets." He struck a mock-warrior pose—fist clenched in one hand, notebook raised high in the other.

"Excuse me?" I asked again, but now making sure I directed my question toward the junkie and not the excited little fat guy.

"Battlebraces," the junkie answered casually. "They're supposed to be an extension of our imagination or some shit, projecting whatever image we deem necessary to fight at the time."

He paused to look me over, and then turned to ask a passerby—who looked like a fellow junkie—if she had a light. After a few seconds passed and several attempts, he found a person with a light, lit the blunt, returned his attention to me, and asked, "How much do you remember?"

He let out a billow of dark green-gray smoke that seemed to trace itself in the image of his words, almost like God was providing me an impromptu closed-captioning to help follow along. It wasn't working.

He took another drag, and with another exhale, asked, "Do you remember a glowing white room?"

C H . 8
EVERYONE
NEEDS A VICE

The question convinced me to walk with them through the Common to converse and enjoy the blunt. The little fat man refused to partake, and almost sneered at us for doing so. Everyone needs a vice.

The junkie and the fat man went on to explain that the little class we were in was actually the heel end of an abduction. They thought it was by aliens at first, but then they began to feel that the government had something to do with it. They weren't sure yet, so they weren't ruling out either possibility. The group in question identified themselves as the Employers, and expressed to all of us that we were chosen to save the world.

Neither the junkie nor the little fat man could explain why we were chosen—just that we had been. Neither one remembered much before the Common, except for a dream about a little, white, pulsating room. They still hadn't told me who they were.

"What do you remember?" the little fat man asked, cutting in front of the junkie to try to get my full attention.

He had an odd face. Like his body, it was neither round nor narrow, and just sat expressionless behind graying black hair that dangled sheepishly down from his high brow. He had small lips, a small nose, and an even smaller set of eyes that sat sunken in his skull and hid within his freckles. With all that said, my guess was that he was about twenty years my senior, which made him close to fifty. It was sad, because his attire reeked of one still living in the basement of his mother's house. The "Member's Only" jacket covering his videogame company t-shirt gave it away.

"What do you mean, what do I remember?" I said sharply. I had no real response at all to give.

"I stated the question as simply as I could. What do you remember before now?" he pressed, but slower this time.

"Well, if you're asking if I remember being invited to a class for junkies on the Common, then no, I don't remember that. The last thing I recall doing was laying on my living room floor, comfortably high."

"Anything else?" the little fat man asked.

"Should there be?"

"He's lying, fatty. Just tell him. We're running out of time," the junkie commanded.

"Yeah, fatty, what's this about? Matter of fact, fuck this!" I said, handing the blunt back to my new junkie best friend. "Thanks for the puff, but I think that will be all for me."

"So, you just going to ignore those veiny gauntlets running up your arms like alien ivy with its own little LCD screen there? And where are you gonna go…Hellokilla?" the junkie yelled as I was walking away.

I turned to face him and the little fat man. "What did you call me?"

"Hellokilla. You see, it says here…" the junkie said, pausing to hold up his left forearm and show me. "It says here on my little screen that your name is Hellokilla." He pointed to a list of names. "I'm MilitantRomeo, and this specimen over here is known as Mr. 4lphaBody. We're your new family. And right now, we have a little family business to discuss, so if you will?" He gestured to himself and Mr. 4lphaBody.

CH. 9
DID I COVER EVERYTHING, FATTY?

The next five minutes were wasted discussing all the things I missed when I mentally tapped out from the weapons training and introduction to my apparent new life.

MilitantRomeo, the junkie, explained, "You see, here…what we got here is a fucked up situation. We are to conduct a bit of a walkabout across this country of ours, hunting each other with alien-grade weapons built for men. Did I cover everything, fatty?" He asked as he turned to Mr. 4lphaBody.

"Hardly." Mr. 4lphaBody snorted. "We have been abducted by forces unknown."

"They're aliens, fatty!" MilitantRomeo corrected loudly. The blunt was clenched between his teeth like a stereotypical drill sergeant's cigar.

"If one cannot prove something, then the logical conclusion is that one cannot disprove it. However, if one is without either claim, then he should remain silent," Mr. 4lphabody snapped back.

"Got some balls on you, don't you?" MilitantRomeo replied. "We'll see when the bullets fly, won't we?"

While they got lost in their spontaneous spousal combustion,

I got lost in my surroundings again. It's hard to grow up in a major metropolitan area and not find some sort of sadistic solace in a random emergency vehicle siren here and there in the brutal summer heat. You come to expect it. Every now and again, there would be more than a few unfortunate souls riding in the ambulance at the same time, creating an eerie orchestra of emergencies among the populace.

But today was different. From every angle, there was a siren. Every street shot flashing lights of red and blue. People began to move in waves from one side of the Common to the other in a shared but unspoken panic. If I didn't know any better, I'd have thought Boston was under attack.

"Listen, like it or not, you are involved in this. Look no further than your arms," the little fat man pleaded. He could hear the sirens, too.

MilitantRomeo was a few paces away, leaning against a light-post and puffing away.

"You need to come with us," Mr. 4lphabody continued. "You don't have to, but I think those sirens mean this whole thing has started, and we need to get equipped."

"Where?" I asked. There wasn't much on my schedule for the day, so humoring this a little longer didn't seem like a bad way to spend it. My fake job search could wait. Plus, ignoring my new friends most likely wouldn't result in understanding what these things clinging to my arms were or how the fuck I could get them off.

"The Employers said the first weapons cache drop would be at our last known residence. I live in Sherborn, and he lives in Andover. What about you?" Mr. 4lphaBody's voice grew more and more frantic, but he fought to keep it under control.

"Framingham." I hadn't lived in Framingham for years, but as far as the government was concerned, I never left.

"Shit. Alright, we have to change plans. MilitantRomeo! We're heading to your house first," Mr. 4lphaBody yelled as he waddled toward him.

"Yeah, you know, about that…" MilitantRomeo began. "We aren't doing this with these fucking names. I didn't even make mine. My kid sister did. It's Drake. You?" Drake asked with a point to me.

"Salt," I replied, agreeing with him completely.

"Well, I made mine, and it means something to me, so I'm keeping it," Mr. 4lphaBody countered.

Drake's glare at Mr. 4lphaBody left me with the immediate impression he was rethinking this partnership, but something held him back.

"Do you have a way to get there?" I asked Drake.

"A few."

Ch. 10
Remarkably Calm for Someone Who Was Just Told He Is Supposed to Be Dead

So, funny story, the plan to get to the first weapons cache drop was to rent a car. We walked to the closest place we could think of—BFRO Car Rentals. Their niche was overpriced and over-the-hill Lexuses and Mercedes and shitty, inconvenient parking spots spread throughout the city. Surprisingly, the inside was a modest setup, with rows of cubicles reminiscent of a Glengarry Glenn Ross sales floor.

Drake approached the first "agent" that looked to be open. The agent, seemingly horrified at being interrupted, held up his index finger to halt Drake from speaking further. He then pointed to his headset to signal the conversation through the earpiece was a bit more important. After thirty seconds, he scribbled a few notes on a small pad of paper, then hung up.

"How may I help you, gentlemen?" the agent asked.

"We need a car," Drake replied bluntly.

"What do you need?"

"What do you have?"

"I just had two Bentleys arrive this morning. I also got a pretty little M2 rested out front. It's gray. You see it? It's nice, huh?" The agent's tongue teetered on hanging from his mouth as he eased into sleazeball mode and leaned back in his office chair.

"What, are you assuming the position? We aren't slutty coeds looking to work a discount," I said, cutting in.

"What's that, bro?" the agent replied.

"How much for the M2?" Drake asked. He was surprisingly focused.

"That depends." The agent shrugged. "How long you need it?"

"Just today."

"One night stand, huh? You need a driver?"

"No, I think one of us can handle it."

"Of course." He smiled and spun in his chair to face his laptop and type a few figures. "I can get you into that M2 for just a shade under a grand right now, and I'll throw in the gas insurance if you sign within the next five minutes."

"I like your style. Draw my papers," Drake commanded comfortably while pulling out his black American Express card. Not too many junkies have that on them.

"Thank you, Mr. Drake."

While the agent was running his card, I leaned toward Drake so only he could hear me.

"Just so we are clear, I had to deposit three dollars the other day to withdraw my last twenty.

"We are in a bit of hurry...." Drake paused, trying to find the agent's name and ignoring my poor man's story.

"It's Karl. Karl with a K," he said before freezing. "There appears to be a problem."

"What seems to be the problem, Karl?"

"The problem is that my computer is telling me that the owner of this card is dead."

"Well, that doesn't seem right, does it, Karl?"

"No, it doesn't."

"What do you suppose we do about it, Karl?"

Drake remained remarkably calm for someone who was just told he is supposed to be dead. I hadn't a clue what that meant, but Mr. 4lphaBody was beginning to have a hard time.

"I don't know."

Karl's hands began to slide, slowing around the edges of his three-quarter desk.

"Where are your hands going, Karl?"

"Nowhere."

"You're lying to me, Karl."

"Yes, I am."

"Why is that, Karl?"

"Standard procedure. I'm not going to check it again."

"I can see that, Karl."

Seeing that nothing would come from testing the battlebraces on this asshole, Drake smiled and nodded. "Do we get a head start?"

"Tell you what," Karl hissed. "How 'bout this? You take this shit back, give it back to your mom's criminal boyfriend who's probably in the mob or some shit, and don't fucking come back and waste any more of my fucking time."

The smile on Drake's face left me a little cold. "I can live with that."

After taking his card back, he turned and headed for the door. We followed, somewhat confused and defeated.

"What just happened?" Mr.4plabody asked.

"Looks like we're dead, fatty," Drake responded as he pushed the door open.

He said nothing more, and proceeded to walk right up to the shining gray M2, parked right out front as promised. He looked down at his battlebraces. He turned his right forearm back and forth to get an even better look. There seemed to be no controls or gauges; just a gel-like plastic that looked like the illegitimate lovechild of a PDA and a tribal flame tattoo.

A dull blue, small, and pointed object materialized from the mouth of Drake's right battlebrace. He shoved it into the keyhole of the car door, turned his fist from side to side until he heard a click, and then slid in.

"How do you feel about being a killer?"

"What the fuck does that mean?" I asked.

"Exactly like it sounds. How do you feel about becoming a killer?"

"What the fuck are you talking about?"

"Obviously, we just stole a car from a car rental company that may respond violently to theft. Now, I don't know about you or the tubby assassin over there, but I know I might not be able to ignore them." Drake held up a battlebrace that was now in the form of a short, fat, bladed object. He held it close to the tip of the blunt hanging from his mouth. To his delight, it seared and lit.

"We didn't steal a car," I fired back, pointing to Mr. 4lpha-Body and myself.

"Fuck all that. We're partners now. Look, I tried to do it the right way, but we all saw how that went. We have to get moving. What choice did I have?"

"Not stealing a car?"

"Hellokilla, Salt, whatever the fuck you want to go by. Look down at your arms, then fucking ask yourself why the computer system said I was dead. Any of this beginning to connect?"

"Doesn't mean we have to become criminals."

"What the fuck difference does it make? Apparently I'm dead. Think I'm the only one with that fate? Can't be criminals if we don't exist."

"Doesn't mean it's the same for me or him,"

"I'm going with him," Mr. 4lphabody announced.

"See! Fat boy is in. Come on, Salt. I just opened this car door and started it with this fucking jellyfish hanging on my right arm, while my left one keeps spitting out names of people I've never fucking heard of. This train is moving, baby. Best get on now and be a passenger before you get plowed on the tracks."

In the back of my head, I could hear a lot of commotion suddenly erupting. I could hear the disappointment from already-disappointed parents over having a criminal for a son if this was all just a big misunderstanding that turned felonious. But that felt wrong.

My heart pounded deep and hard. I couldn't breathe. The world was turning in the opposite direction for me. I wanted to run, or use the battlebraces on these two for putting me in this position. I was fucked. Just being associated with a car theft was enough to get a young black man convicted in my fair city of Boston.

I could hear all that, but even louder with each passing second, I could hear more sirens at one time than I had ever heard in my life. They climbed over each other like crabs escaping a barrel.

Time was up. I had to make a decision. I barreled around the M2 and hopped in shotgun.

C H . 1 1
A NEW LOT IN LIFE

Drake lived in a small, exclusive pocket of North Andover, tucked away in some hills lining the northern side of town with picture-perfect lawns. His house was at the center of a cul-de-sac that was the flagship of this posh neighborhood. I said "was" because in the place of his last known residence, we found a crater the size of a hockey rink.

Drake didn't hesitate when he parked the car and got out to look around his street. After giving the area a survey, he nodded once to himself. He then began to march toward the weapons cache placed in the middle of the crater, but halted when he saw the presenter from the Common.

Instead of cowering or taking the opportunity to engage him on what was going on, Drake continued toward the weapons cache to check it over.

The presenter and one of his large companions walked directly in front of us. He seemed relaxed, except for his hands being clasped behind his back. He looked as though he had been waiting long but patiently, even though he came out of nowhere. His face was emotionless, but an odd sense of pride oozed from him, as if he were pleased at our arrival.

C H . 1 2
Smoke 'Em If You Got 'Em

"Good afternoon, gentlemen," he said like he hadn't a worry in the world.

"Do I know you?" I asked.

"I believe so. No matter, I know you." He looked over to Drake. "And you as well, Mr. Drake."

Drake ignored the acknowledgement and continued to make his way toward the center of the crater.

"Congratulations, gentlemen," the man continued. "Most subjects out of your group didn't even make it this far."

"What the fuck is going on? Who are you?" I demanded.

"The question is, who are you supposed to be now?" the man corrected.

Drake had finally worked his way up the mound of rubble to the weapons cache. It was resting on what appeared to be the remains of a kitchen counter with precisely cut edges, but only a square foot of it. It was a sort of makeshift monument to Drake's last residence. He quickly examined the contents, then closed the bag and made his way back.

"Let me be brief," the mysterious man said. "You all have a lot to do. Mr. Bresnik, would you like to join us? This concerns you as well, Mr. Drake."

"How do you know our names?" I asked. "What the fuck—"

"What answer will move you, Mr. Salt? What question can you ask with what little you know to satisfy your curiosity? I'd venture none. But I understand your primal need for information, even if you wouldn't know truth from lie. It's part of the reason why we are here."

"Who is 'we'? Can you fucking tell me that?"

"All the cars lined up and down this street, yeah.... Who they belong to?" Drake asked, pointing to the cars with the muzzle of the gun he was now holding.

The cartoon images from the lesson in the Common were actually quite accurate. I was beginning to remember more than I had thought I learned from that afternoon.

"It's called the battleautomatic, Mr. Salt. They come as a pair. With its rapid firing rate, it will shred an enemy's activeskin in seconds." He paused to look Drake in the eyes. "The cars belong to everyone you know, Mr. Drake."

"Yeah, where are they?"

"They're dead, MilitantRomeo, or Drake, or whatever the fuck your name is," I said. "Aren't they, you bald fuck?"

"Quite astute, Mr. Salt. Though I must confess that I am a bit taken aback from such harsh words from one who remains hairless as well."

"Why are they dead?" Drake asked.

"Because, gentlemen, in order for you to proceed, you must first not exist. And how do you create a walking poltergeist? You kill everyone who could confirm they exist. A thousand apologies, but it was necessary." He seemed like he was trying to be sincere.

"You sick fuck..." I whispered.

"You did this to all of us?" Mr. 4lphaBody choked.

"Yeah, fatty," Drake cut in.

"As I said, it was necessary. Mr. Salt, you still don't know what's going on, do you? Why you are here?"

"No, can't say I do."

It was hard to focus. My knees grew weak and threatened to give out. I couldn't stop looking at the crater that once was Drake's house. The reality was finally setting in. My family and everyone I ever knew was dead because of me. How do you say goodbye to everyone you know? How many tears would have to flow before you'd cried enough for everyone you loved? I felt the ungodly guilt. It crushed me; lungs first, then heart and brain.

Then came the rage.

"Now that I have your attention, shall I proceed? Good. In case your memory hasn't fully returned, for mere reference's sake, I am Mr. Polite. I am but a humble herald for those responsible for this contest, if you will—the Employers. I am here to remind you that you have a lot of work to do, gentlemen. The contest, as it were, has already begun. You mustn't lag about."

"And do what?" Mr. 4lphaBody screamed, to the point that his eyes grew bloodshot and his stature crumbled over, beaten from all the impossible information coming like bullets from a firing squad.

"I know all this might make it difficult to remember, poor Mr. Bresnik, but you—along with a select group of lucky individuals—have been chosen to test the weapons your compatriot is holding at present, along with those nifty gauntlets you all are fashioned with. Battlebraces! The left one has your navguide—a map of your surroundings, accompanied by omnipotent tactical information, including but not limited to an identification indicator for both combatant and compatriot. This data is accurate out to one kilometer. However, this feature is a beta, so we ask that you all respect those limitations and maintain contact with your teammates up to those limited parameters. Data collected must be consistent, of course. Failure to do so will classify the lost teammate as a combatant. The discarded teammate will no longer be part of a team, while the remaining members will incur steep penalties."

"We're a team?" Drake growled.

"Yes, of course. That is what Mr. Bresnik selected upon being released."

Drake and I both turned to look at Mr. 4lphaBody with the notion of "What the fuck?"

He met our stare with a shrug and a look back that reeked of "what are you going to do about it?"

"When did we start getting choices?" I asked.

"Would you like to go back to the Common and try again?"

"Maybe," Drake fired back. "You keep saying 'released.' Released from what?"

"Does it need a name? We took you, equipped you with those gauntlets, and activeskin—" Mr. Polite paused just long enough for his giant companion to articulate the point with a bullet to Mr. 4lphaBody's head. The force knocked Mr. 4lphaBody back, but didn't kill him or even draw blood. "—the reason why Mr. Bresnik is still with us this moment, mind you. And then released you back into the wild to hunt each other. You can call it what you will."

"For weapons testing?" Drake repeated.

"Correct, Mr. Drake. Now, if I may…" Mr. Polite continued on explaining what we were equipped with.

"How is this possible?" I asked. "How are you doing this? This can't be—"

"Real? Mr. Salt, I suspect that should you survive this all, the notion of what is or is not real will be drastically different."

"But why us?" I asked once more.

"Why not? Would it matter if I told you that you were selected at random, or that there was something so unique within you? What if I told you that despite having completed over hundred special op missions, the United States Marine Corps dishonorably discharged your new friend, Mr. Drake, because of…what, exactly?"

"Classified," Drake said through a giant, shit-eating grin that felt more scary than congenial.

"Classified," Mr. Polite repeated. He returned the smile. "Perhaps, Mr. Salt, it is that you are all very good at keeping secrets. View it as a blessing to witness what is to become of this world, firsthand and with VIP access."

"I view it as someone telling me I have to go kill people after that person just told me he is responsible for killing everyone I love."

"Not just love, Mr. Salt. As of right now, I and the gentlemen that accompany you at present are the only souls who know you exist. Anyone who even knew of your life is no longer alive."

"That's impossible," I whispered. "You would've had to have killed over—"

"20,135 people...roughly. For you, Mr. Drake, 79,378. And for Mr. Bresnik, whose legend reaches far and wide in the online gaming realm, and really the reason we went with using gamer-tags for your personas, had over 1.9 million people attached to his existence."

"You killed over two million people just to create this 'contest'?"

"Oh, much, much more than that. Over 2.1 million for the three of you. It's closer to a billion worldwide, with all the subjects accounted for. Now, there is no time limit to your task at hand, but I can't promise the Employers will always be patient," Mr. Polite said as he ignored me and proceeded to tell us what he was there to say, with or without emotional feedback. "You'll find everything you need in the caches. My apologies for the loss of your loved ones. They will not have died in vain. Your country needs you. Happy hunting, Godspeed," he pronounced with a halfhearted bow of his head.

"What if we refuse?"

"Well, Mr. Salt, Salt, Hellokilla—whatever you fancy to call yourself—in about two minutes, you'll have your answer. See you soon, gentlemen."

"When does this end?" Drake asked.

"When there is just one of you."

"Meaning what?"

"Kill as many as the others as you want, but this ends where there is just one like you."

"So much for teammates."

"Wait, what does that mean?" Mr. 4lphaBody asked, finally gaining some control of himself.

"We're eventually going to have to kill each other, fatty," Drake said.

"Why are you doing this?" Mr. 4lphaBody screamed.

"Is that the question you should be asking right now, Mr. Bresnik?" Polite said as he and his freakish companion turned and disappeared around the house to the left of Drake's crater.

We didn't chase to see where they went. Moments later, we heard a deep wail of smooth-running machinery followed by gusts of wind from behind the house.

The lack of sound of everything else was beginning to get to me in a way I could never fathom before that day. I expected to hear the neighborhoods around us alive with excitement, curiosity, and fear. I expected to hear emergency vehicles en route to investigate the presumably violent removal of a residence. A news helicopter to give it a look over, or by God, even just cars passing by on neighboring streets.

But nothing. Absolutely nothing.

There was a huge fucking crater the size of a small pond in place of a house in this once-snooty neighborhood, but not so much as a squad car to investigate why. Any modicum of hope that this was a cruel joke was destroyed.

CH. 13
WHAT WAS ONCE THE INSPIRATION OF ANY HALLMARK CARD WAS NOW THE MUSE TO JOHN CARPENTER'S NIGHTMARES

Drake immediately went to the garage of an adjacent house and broke the window of the side door. Once inside, he just stood in awe of his booty: a shining two door Maybach coupe to make the ride to our next destination something special.

"I never liked this guy," Drake said as he moved to grab the keys hanging by the door to the house.

"Wait, there's only two seats," Mr. 4lphaBody quickly complained. "We have to find a car with enough seats for everyone. I mean.... I'm not getting in there."

By this time, Drake had already made a comfortable space for himself in the passenger side. He outfitted his area with all his weapons for quick and certain access—best reason I could think of for shoving weapons between the seats and doors. He hadn't even winced a shred of sorrow for the loss of everyone who knew he existed. Meanwhile, I'd puked twice and Mr. 4plhaBody was a sobbing mess that I swear slid over to the garage on his own mucus.

"What is your name?" Drake snapped.

"Mr. 4lphaBody," he answered, confused.

"No, you fat fuck, your name. The name someone once called you before you had let go of reality. The name on your birth certificate. And if you say your hero name, I'll try this battlebrace out on your back."

"Lenny. Lenny Bre—" Mr. 4lphaBody began to add defeated. He probably had never won a fight or confrontation in his life.

"Forget about the names or all the fucking virtual conquests you've done. This is fucking real and we are running out of time. Just listen. We're next door to a crater that once was known as my house. It looks as if WWIII has started in Boston because of this game, contest, whatever the fuck you want to call it. And I'm not waiting for someone to drop hell at my feet with only my weapon cache, so you get in the fucking trunk or you fucking go at this alone," Drake said calmly while tapping Lenny's head with one of the weapons.

"But—"

"Salt, drive," said Drake, interrupting. The weapon was now aimed at Lenny's head. We both stepped back from the sudden surge of yellow liquid making its way from Lenny's feet to the garage opening.

Lenny was climbing into the trunk when Drake's arm began to glow. I had forgotten about that part of the left battlebrace.

"The navguide," Lenny said, hushed. His eyes grew the size of saucers.

"See this?" Drake asked, tapping the section of his battlebraces that was all lit up. "We don't have any fucking time. You want to live?"

"Yes."

"Then get in the fucking trunk," Drake instructed.

We pushed Lenny into the trunk. I got behind the wheel while Drake hopped in shotgun. He smiled and turned toward me. "We need to go."

His left arm was ablaze now. It showed that out of seven names, four were about to be right on top of us. The thunderclap of firearms moved closer and closer. Seconds now felt like hours.

I had never felt the impact of explosions in my general vicinity, but I was almost certain that was what I was hearing and feeling. I could feel the walls of the garage beginning to tremble and shudder around me, before they began to slowly rip away. At the same time, bright light filled the room, accompanied late by fire and heat that would overwhelm someone in seconds. Tools and books flew off the falling shelves. Through it all, I could hear Lenny kicking and screaming from the dark of the trunk. Drake already had his battlerifle cocked and ready to go.

I reached to press the ignition button. Power from underneath my seat roared throughout the car. Before today, the fastest car I'd driven was a Lexus. This Maybach's median speed was a hundred; it was hard to fight back the arousal from possibly achieving 200 mph at least once before I died.

The instant the car started, the garage doors blew off as the rest of the structure began to explode. I pulled out through the debris and fire. The car screeched onto the street, screaming around the corner and into the neighborhood's main road.

We were immediately met by some old lady, maybe in her sixties, driving like Mad Max down the street in an old Bronco. A guy about my age rode shotgun. He was halfway out the window, with us in the sights of what appeared to be the rocket launcher from the presentation in the Common. The whole thing was so large the blackness of the barrel seemed to stretch into infinity.

They rammed into our passenger side, forcing Drake back into the car. Without hesitation, he switched his firing hand with his free hand and launched his fist through the window. A glowing blade extended from his wrist and into the woman's side.

She screamed in agony as the Bronco violently veered away. The young man riding shotgun was thrown off-balance from her sudden pain. Slamming against the roof, he hung out the window, dazed.

"Keep your distance!" Drake yelled over the roar of air and the engine.

The task was harder than it sounded. We were racing through the picture-perfect streets of the affluent neighborhoods of North Andover. We were a good two miles away from Drake's crater, so just far enough to be unaware. Little kids played in their yards, happy and unsuspecting. Old couples proudly worked on their own yards as soccer moms unloaded groceries from the back of their choice luxury SUVs. It had to have been a Saturday. Even the sun seemed brighter. The Bronco went barreling into all of that. What was once the inspiration for any Hallmark card was now the muse to John Carpenter's nightmares.

Drake leaned out the window and opened fire. What wasn't already killed by the Bronco was by his hand. He was accurate, but we were going around these curvy suburban roads at over eighty miles per hour—he was bound to miss. It was clear he also didn't care about anything, least of all innocent life.

My attention was drawn to a classic Camaro flying down the street in the rearview mirror. I ignored it—until bullets found my arms and neck. Oddly, it didn't hurt as much as getting hit with a bullet should have. Matter of fact, aside from a glint of light washing over me no longer than a blink, I almost didn't know it was happening. Then the pain came, and came swift. Numbing at first, then turning to the slow sensation of your skin being torn apart.

Taking his time, Drake finally found the Bronco's sweet spot, sending a small explosion through the back of the truck. The blast lifted the truck back-first into the air, sending it crashing into some house's cozy nook.

Drake saw the Camaro and opened fire on the passenger, who

looked like someone's father. The man's face was still strained from immense emotional distress. I was willing to bet he still was thinking of the loss of his entire living identity, too.

The driver couldn't have been more than sixteen. His pale white knuckles death-gripped the steering wheel, like someone would when forced to test what little driving knowledge they had in a life-or-death situation. His frail physique, lost in his helplessly baggy clothes, begged of the most annoying online n-bomb-dropping suburban white kid, ever so brave thanks to the protection of online identities.

Drake began to aim for the tires, sending the Camaro swerving uncontrollably down the street. The man firing from the passenger seat began to place erratic return fire. Houses were greeted with rounds from his battleshotgun, riddling the bodies of the innocent.

"Massacre" would only begin to describe what the past two minutes had brought and what could only be promised in the very abrupt future.

The Camaro's fender hit our car directly in the back driver side, sending us into a flat spin.

Drake leaned further out of the window to get a better sight of the car heading right for us as we spun. Trying to mimic my best Bruce Willis driving maneuvers, I threw the car into reverse to keep the distance between us manageable for Drake—something I was all too willing to do since the car belonged to someone who most likely was dead.

Without missing a second, Drake began to open fire on the entire car, sending it into a small explosion like the Bronco before it. Then he let loose on the driver to stop their control of the car.

The kid tried to swerve to avoid Drake's aim but, he was soon killed by the combination of the engine exploding and Drake's fire. The shooter was so disoriented from the explosion and the unpredictable movement of the car that his weapons were no threat. Their vehicle finally came to a stop, dead in the middle of the street.

"Stop the car," Drake said, looking right at me.

Once the car stopped, Drake handed me both the automatics, then grabbed his battleshotgun and got out. He had his rifle, too, slung across his back.

"Was it skill, just the grace of God, or luck of a fool? Doesn't matter. We are about to find out," he said before getting out of the car.

The poor man still looked confused from the whole situation. It's a lot to ask an individual to accept the death of his existence, while participating in the killing of someone else who presumably had gone through the same thing at the same time.

Drake looked at his navguide and held his right index and middle fingers in the air to signify how many were left in our general vicinity. His head never stopped surveying the surroundings. Dishonorably discharged or not, he was still a trained soldier.

When he reached the man hanging out the Camaro's door, Drake wasted no time in raising the barrel of his shotgun to the man's head, pausing for no longer than a breath before pulling the trigger. He then turned and began to cautiously retrace his steps back to my position.

"Why did you pause?" I asked. It didn't fit his behavior thus far.

"He was saying something," Drake answered coldly.

"What did he say?"

"'My name is Scott Larken. Thank you.'"

C H . 1 4
ThisIsWhyIHateYou

New Mexico, 2007

"You didn't believe that shit?" Sunday cut in.

"What? The guy's name?"

"No. About this all being about weapons testing for some powerful organization."

"Why? You didn't?"

"Fuck no! Only the cannon fodder believed that, and they were weeded out long ago. Goddamn, how have you two survived?"

"You keep saying that."

"It's just amazing, that's all. What happened next? You saw it, right? The end?"

The commotion outside began to quiet down a bit. It seemed like Drake had respected the bouncer's firm requests, or killed the entire place. Coin toss most days.

"If by 'the end,' you mean my house, then yes. I saw that next."

"And?"

"And what?"

"What did you feel?"

"Are you really fucking here for that?"

"Well I'm damn sure not here to advise you on proper oral hygiene."

Raucous knocking on the door interrupted our mental chess game, but was cut short with a shot from Sunday's sidearm.

"Just killing normals for wanting to piss, huh?"

She smirked. "You sure that's a normal?"

"Why are you here?"

"You should be dead. Your friend should be caught. Yet the two of you have made it so far that you have pissed off Samytus without even thinking for a second that all of this is a bit fucking much for a fucking weapons test."

"I said I did."

C H . 1 5
N O T H I N G
FRIENDLY ABOUT IT

Boston, 2006

Looking back, I could see how it looked like Hell across Boston. If small skirmishes like this had brought this much catastrophe, a full-on battle would mirror that area's own personal Armageddon.

Pillars of smoke from neighborhoods lining the highway rose up to the sky in silent cries of untold anguish. It was hard to escape that whatever this was had started. As we travelled down 93 South I could only imagine this was what war-torn countries looked like on a good day with slightly fewer vehicle-littered interstates. Some cars looked perfectly fine, while others looked like they had exploded.

Glancing at me while he navigated the highway, Drake asked, "Do you believe this shit now?"

He then handed me a spliff. He wasn't bothered or worried, at least, not by any outward expression. His demeanor and the weed made me feel that this was already routine to him, like we were merely picking up a package at his house.

I wasn't sure how to answer that, so I took a deep, lung-burning drag and just stared out the window, trying my hardest to swallow this whole thing down.

My grief over what I had just taken part in moved, without apology, to the death of everyone in my life. My mother and father, my sister, my nephews, my aunts and uncles and cousins, my friends, my exes, my old teachers and coaches, my everybody—all I'd ever cared for.

I fought against the crippling shock that came from thinking for even a moment that all this was true. But then it occurred to me I was already in shock. I was already numb.

There is no way to prepare for such a loss. There is no amount of grieving that can make you feel you've properly respected the passing of a loved one, let alone many loved ones. No amount that can make you feel you've done enough.

I could have cried, but I knew I didn't have enough tears. I could have asked God a series of questions, but I knew I wouldn't hear any answers. Funny enough, if by some miracle I did get answers, I knew I wouldn't be able to handle the information. I was damned to the anguish I embodied.

I was so deep in pain I found myself fighting against the notion that there was nothing I could do with the agony if I chose to exist for something more than to grieve all I'd lost until I was dead and gone as well. No. I'd say fuck that and grieve when I die.

I didn't know this right away—not in the sense of knowing stepping in front of a speeding train is antithetical to wanting to live. It was more the automatic knowing that comes from the same place that tells us to gasp for breath after being submerged too long. But it didn't matter, because I had already drowned. I was already dead.

"We have to make a stop," Drake said suddenly, breaking the silence.

This can't be real, I thought. I was driving on autopilot while Drake comfortably rested in the passenger seat. Sans Lenny's kicking and screaming, the only sound was the roar of the engine and scrapes from the twisted metal and plastic that clung to our car's mangled chassis. Strained from being launched into a deadly makeshift version of a neighborhood demolition derby, the engine became unbearably loud, but still felt strong. It was almost inconceivable to believe what this car had just gone through. Can't imagine a consumer report written to gauge a vehicle's ability to handle itself in a combat situation, but so far so good.

"Where? For what?" I struggled to ask, caught in deep thought.

"I want to get some weed."

"You're kidding, right? You have to be fucking kidding me, MilitantRomeo."

"Alright. First, cut that shit. It's Drake, and you're Salt. Enough with the fucking superhero avatar names shit. I didn't even make that fucking name. My kid sister did when I was away, and I was too cheap to create another one to play around on that dumb fucking videogame machine. You can go by whatever you want, but fucking call me Drake."

He had a point. There was enough to wrap my head around without assuming a real-life persona of my online avatar.

"Salt will be fine," I said. "But are you fucking serious about weed? It seems we have more pressing matters."

"Why? If I'm going to die, I'm going out high."

"Not that I don't want to smoke sometime before I see the end, but can I at least get my weapon shit before you get all kinds of elation?"

"Listen. Get the panties undone. Look at it logically, if that's even possible in light of all this. Boston is, for all intents and purposes, under attack. They don't know what's going on, so I can only assume their emergency employees are stretched beyond any hopes of conducting and completing any effective daily standard operations. We will pass Boston on the way to Framingham. We just take a quick, unscheduled tour of Boston Metro's evidence room while they scatter to help the helpless and scared. Imagine your selection power." Drake grinned.

"And you don't think this is, at any level, a dumb and useless risk?"

"Maybe, but with dumb and useless risks come favorable rewards. What's the worst, we kill a cop?"

"And you're fine with that—senseless killing of people that don't have to be involved in any of this."

"Salt, I probably just killed six people who had nothing to do with any of this, and whom I would have most certainly not have been in contact with if it weren't for this fucking game. And after I accidentally killed the first innocent while I was trying to defend myself—my guilt went limp with that person. Whether by God's will or the devil's design, my actions are with two shadows from here on out."

"Are you finished, Reverend?" I asked, mocking his thinly-veiled bible reference.

"Only if I have to be."

"Not that I disagree with you, but I don't fucking accept going out of my way to kill those who have nothing to do with this."

"Then who says we have to kill any police? They might not even be there to try to stop us. And if they are, they might reconsider what's important in their lives when they notice their bullets falling at our feet." Drake held up one of his weapons. "You noticed yet that these high-powered Godzilla-killers rip through everything and everyone save us? That it took some doing to take down granny and her faggy boy-toy assassin?"

"It's called activeskin!" a voice yelled from the back.

"The fuck was that?" I asked in shock, only to remember we left Lenny in the trunk. What a trooper.

"Fuck you! Get me out of here!" Lenny screamed.

"Soon!" Drake fired back. He turned his attention back to me. "You don't remember shit, do you?"

"Sorry, guess I was a bit preoccupied."

"With fucking what? We were abducted, drugged, and forced to watch their preschool production seminar on weapons training. These weapons." He held up the weapons cache. It was almost like a clown car with its ability to squeeze all those weapons in.

"It's real simple. All the weapons start with the word 'battle.' So, for example, battleshotgun." Drake pulled out a rectangular object about a foot and a half in length. The barrel was rectangular, as well. "This fucker will eat activeskin in two rounds. Very fun."

He paused to pull out the other automatic. "Battleautomatics. All the weapons are light. Real light, actually. But these little fuckers fire at a minigun's rate. I think Polite said something like a hundred rounds from the automatics, the sidearms, and the battlerifle will deactivate the activeskin."

"Why did you go AWOL?" I asked.

"Who said this was going to become a psych session? Let's stay focused, fucking grasshopper."

"Motivating."

"I got a book deal. Moving on. You got the battlesniper rifle, or BSR, cause who the fuck wants to say 'battlesniper rifle' over and over? Not gonna lie, this one makes me a little hard. Just a little."

"You're taking quite well to your new lot in life."

I could feel Drake staring at me in the same way he did earlier—reading me, checking to see where the cracks were. Ignoring my question, he pulled out a small, foot-by-foot box.

"This little beauty was titled the devastational cube. I can't show you now, but trust me, this little rocket launcher is centuries away from anything we have now. Shit, all this stuff is, but according to the little presentation, this fucker will topple a skyscraper with a few well-placed rounds at the foundation. Best part is, aside from the fact that only a direct hit from this will kill a combatant like us, this thing doesn't need to reload with standard ammo. Like the sidearms, it uses elements found in the Earth's atmosphere to develop rounds. Of course, for something this big, reloading takes some time. But good to know."

"Like fucking watching hacks chop it up on Iron Chef," I said, amazed at his wonderment.

He formed a small blade to drive his point home. "I'm gonna have some fun with these. Talk about this is my weapon and this is my gun," he said while grabbing his crotch. His eyes shined with childlike excitement.

"By the way, I wasn't fucking kidding about getting more drugs." Drake was smiling, but there was nothing friendly about it.

C H . 1 6
POLICE, THIEVES, AND ARISTOCRATIC GIANTS

Drake had a point—about the drugs, that is. If every moment I faced could be my last, going out on top of a government-seized grade-A green magic THC flying carpet wouldn't be all that bad. Might have room for little buddies like cocaine, shrooms, tanks of LSD, hash, meth, Vicodin, OCs, poppers, and that little bitch, X. Just to name a few.

Even with accidents littering the roads, it didn't take much time getting to BPD Metro Station. Parking right in front—thanks to the absence of Chief O'Hurley's town car—we walked right in.

Drake was right. It was a ghost town in the precinct. The sheer annoyance of the constant tone and pitch of all the phones ringing caused a low humming sound in the ears that numbingly dug at one's senses. Utter insanity would have been a welcome change, but we pressed on.

The station was a mess. Desks and shelves were upheaved and disheveled. The classic black and white checkered linoleum floor held so many papers, folders, and flipped over chairs, it was like walking on some fucked-up dessert tray for aristocratic giants. Looking at the walls, I could tell gunfire had been discharged. That, along with the smoke-heavy atmosphere in a non-smoking building. There was some blood scattered about, but no bodies, and not enough blood to suggest many died—or even one, for that matter. Matter of fact, the place just looked like shit.

The lights that survived the apparent battle joined in the illusion, creating a rhythmic glow normally found in the long fluorescent bulbs warming up in a forgotten factory. Now, I was begging for insanity.

Time took on an entirely new meaning. It felt like it was constantly dissolving and reestablishing its presence in my subconscious. What was troubling was that it felt missed and welcomed.

Drake had a nose for drugs. His lust for sharing realities between sober and fucked-up was greater than I thought humanly possible. I think it was the only way he could handle people.

The drug seizure room was on floor B2. The police info center was very helpful. Apparently, the employees needed a little "you are here" every now and then. Seeing how the place wasn't exactly tiptop, we decided to take the stairs.

"You know what I can't stop thinking about?" Drake asked playfully, breaking the silence as we casually walked toward the stairway entrance to B2.

"How much you can carry?" I replied.

"No, Maui-wo—"

Drake's voice was absorbed by the thunderous crack that echoed through the stairway from behind us. Drake, in pain, clutched at his back from reflex and the sheer shock of being shot point-blank by a 12-gauge. Wasting little time, we both turned to see who fired. There, standing proudly with the smoking shotgun, stood the most stereotypical old black janitor I had ever seen.

"Did you just get shot by the conductor from Silver Bullet?" I asked in absolute horror—not because he shot Drake, but because he wasn't scared Drake was still standing. He appeared to be just very pissed. His lip quivered, but it was from ungodly meanness.

"I'm a custodian, dick," the old man said.

He added a pump of the 12-gauge just to be clear in his intentions. He had an unrealistic confidence about him. It was downright disconcerting.

"Whoa, whoa, whoa. Don't you think you should rethink your strategy, sir?" I pleaded.

"Fuck him, Salt! He just shot me," Drake said, becoming more and more pissed by the amount of time gone by before the old man at least got slapped.

"I know, Drake, but he's probably just scared."

"I ain't scared," the old man loudly corrected. We could only step back as he completed his statement of hostility with spit at our toes.

"Not helping, Ole Roscoe," I said.

"James," he corrected again. He grabbed his nametag to help make his point.

"It says Jenkins," I defended.

"Well, it's Cleophus Oswald Jenkins, but folks call me James," the old man scoffed.

"Does it matter?" I pleaded again with hands out. If I could just get him to shut up long enough for Drake to calm down, then this night might not be his last, I hoped.

"Fuck that, you little piss-ant," the old man snapped. "I'll eat him up."

He hung his chin out, begging to get punched. Then, without any warning, he came charging and drilled the butt of the shotgun directly into the crown of Drake's nose.

Drake fell back in pain, blood running freely from his nose. His eyes never closed, but instead fixed on the old man. The old man tried to retreat, but Drake was already up with one hand firmly gripped around his neck. The other came up in an upward motion toward ole James's head in the shape of an abnormally large medieval pike's head.

I grabbed Drake's arm. "You'll heal. You don't have to do this. I think he understands now."

"Arrrrgghhhh!" Drake yelled as he dropped ole James to the ground. He turned to storm down the hallway, toward the drug seizure room. "The next one dies!"

"Yeah, cause I was just about to get in that ass," James postured triumphantly.

"The fuck he say?" Drake snapped back, turning halfway before trying even harder to forget the ordeal.

"Enough. James, we're going to steal some weed and some other shit. Maybe roll some shit up and blaze here, you know—for the memory," I began to explain.

He stared blankly at me. A moment ago, even his shitty job was going to be missed, and now the man that saved him was laying out his intentions—all for him to digest. I can't imagine how it felt.

"Boy, I don't know what the fuck that just meant," he said.

"Would you like to drop your shotgun there, that clearly will result in no one dying except for you, and smoke some police-seized weed with us?" I asked as plainly as I could.

"Well shit, that's alright. Cool."

C H . 1 7
HAVES AND HAVE NOTS

New Mexico, 2007

"You two assholes were told you need to hunt others like you, immediately take out a wealthy suburb—demonstrating that no matter what this was, you were in real danger—and decide robbing a police precinct for drugs was the next best action?" Sunday interrupted. The look of disgust, horror, and shock compounded with disbelief across her face.

"Don't forget smoking with ole James."

"No, of course. How could I? Ole James." Sunday sarcastically punctuated with a slap across her knee.

"Ole James."

"Fuck you, Salt."

I smirked. "Don't hold back, now."

"I'm really starting to reevaluate how I survived so far."

"How did you? Better still, why do you care about Drake and me so much? Is there truth to what Polite said? This only ends when there is one of us?"

"One of you."

"No clue what that means."

"Not yet. Tell me more. What did you see next?"

"Okay, I'm done. You came out of your little witch portal or whatever the fuck it's called to come visit me. You keep telling me that we are about to make a mistake, but—"

"Enough with the bitching and just fucking tell me what you saw next. You wouldn't understand me if I gave you the answers to your questions right now. You need to see it."

"How do I know you have any answers?"

"Who's got the witch portal, or whatever the fuck you call it?"

C H . 1 8
SUNDAY'S BEST
WAITING FOR DEATH

Somewhere between Massachusetts and Connecticut, 2006

Colors, colors, colors. We were fucked up. The violent blend of lights and blurred images that come with the speed we were traveling played out through my own television show, otherwise known as the view to my reality through eyes barely open enough to register those images flashing by. Glancing at the speedometer, I could see we were floating at about ninety-two miles per hour, surprisingly smooth in a stolen, unmarked police cruiser.

Streetlights became shooting stars. Time became theoretical, to the point that it almost didn't exist. My mouth was so dry I could spit cotton. We took everything. OxyContin. Vacating. X. I was fighting my stomach's need to release the toxins the drugs love to leave.

However, my mind was in a place no element could touch, not even pain. At the moment, the THC in my system was, remarkably, playing the role of sobering agent against the combination of mind-altering/psycho-controllable substances ingested in bulk. Necessary, considering the biggest tragedy my life will ever face sent me into a thought process I had never known. Feeling such a sudden and massive loss, in such proximity of occurrence, was a feeling not yet discovered.

Most of my life since the Battles began, my days remained in an almost comatose trance. Time held no bearing for me anymore. I fought to answer the instinct to survive, but I had no will to live. Complete and utter emotional numbness is the only way to describe losing everyone you ever loved while being the cause, indirectly or not.

Drake basically drove while Lenny and I rode. It felt like Drake did his best to shield us from battles. Maybe he thought we weren't ready. I think he was right.

By that point, we had fallen backward into several battles, narrowly escaping death each time. We weren't warriors—at least, Lenny and I weren't—but we survived by the grace of whatever god there is and the sick sense of humor it had for us.

Maybe that was why I didn't ask or wonder why Drake took a detour off the highway and cruised through the little towns often forgotten in this country. It wasn't like we had a map to follow or a timeline to meet.

"Pull over, I feel sick," Lenny announced from the backseat. If it weren't for his periodic comment of disgust for my and Drake's drug use, you wouldn't have even known he was there.

"Relax, fatty. Just take deep breaths," Drake said. His assurances were met with Lenny's puke flying from the back and splashing on the dashboard. The car swerved to a sudden halt in the middle of the road.

"Okay, I guess we need a new car," Drake said as he put it in park. I thought Lenny was going to get battlebraced for sure, but remarkably, Drake remained almost stoic. Perhaps the drugs had their place after all.

We stepped out onto a desolate street in the middle of nowhere. The entire neighborhood looked the same—like the backdrop of a poorly-produced movie lot from an unimaginative set director. All the cars rested safely in single-lane driveways, but there was no traffic in the streets. There were no people walking down the sidewalks or children playing in their yards. Not even the breeze moving through the trees carried a sound. There was nothing, just extreme and frightening silence. It felt like we were at the edge of our apparent universe.

It was just your everyday stroll through a ghost town—until we heard someone shriek, "Hellokilla!"

The shriek belonged to a little girl standing behind us. No older than nine, she stood defiantly in the middle of the street with a devastational cube fully extended and ready for death. Sporting pigtails and a dress meant for Sunday's best, the little girl, who must have been waiting for us, was the scariest thing I had ever seen.

C H . 1 9
MY PRETTY LITTLE HESITATION AT THE EDGE OF THE UNIVERSE

Waiting until her eyes could confirm her navguide readings, she slowly lifted her arm, raising the fully extended devastational cube with little effort. She taunted us with her incredible strength by cheerfully swaying side to side with the rocket launcher but refraining from firing. Felines do the same thing while toying with their prey.

With the most evil leer I'd seen in my short life, she swung her other arm out from behind her, exposing prize #2—battlerifle. Her giggle echoed through the streets like she were a giant. Then, without warning, she opened fire.

The little girl was relentless. Her strength was amazing. Time stood still as this demonic child opened up attack after attack. We tried to find cover, be it a parked car or the side of a house. She destroyed each barrier one by one just to fuck with us, never giving us even a second to gain our bearings.

"This little twat is on her own," Drake yelled over the sound of his roaring battlerifle as he continued to return fire. "Tubby—you alright?"

"Fuck you!" Lenny screeched from behind a minivan.

"Listen, you fat—"

An explosion ripped through the air, cutting Drake's words off.

The little girl had launched a devastational rocket directly at Lenny's minivan. Lenny was sent through the air and crashed through the bay windows of a house behind the vehicle.

"Holy shit.... Move!" Drake hollered while putting his hand on my back to push me in the direction he was thinking.

We got across the street, in between houses and out of her sight. Bullets outlined our every step. She was still playing with us.

"I don't care if this little twat is pintsize, she's gotta go down in a big way," Drake growled. His amusement at the situation had taken a toxic right turn toward violent hatred. "Cut behind these houses and hit her from the side. I'll wait till you draw her fire, then open up on her from the front. If we do this right, we'll get this little bitch before she can fire off another rocket." Drake's hands waved to illustrate his instructions.

I hurried through the various backyards. I hadn't a clue of what I was doing or how to do it; I just ran, hurdling over playschool playsets and cheap, six-inch-deep kiddy pools every other yard.

She met me in between houses. We stood within a foot of each other, but neither of us spoke. We just stared blankly.

Then, with another frightening giggle, she leapt up into the air, landing her feet on my chest. She pushed off with her left foot while her right connected perfectly with my chin, sending me staggering back. Wasting no time, she launched herself back into the air and landed directly on my chest again—before my back even touched the ground.

Once we landed, she leaned back, then came forward to expose three elongated, skeletal blades from each battlebrace, Wolverine-style. She dug them directly into both of my shoulders. I went blind from the pain surging through me like an electric current.

Screaming, I sent the little girl flying back into the air. I searched the ground for all the weapons that fell after getting dropkicked by my new nemesis as her giggles provided the soundtrack to my losing efforts. The battleshotgun, lying slightly closer than the rest, became my only choice. I fought back the pain overwhelming my senses and grabbed the weapon, turning to pull the trigger right as she began to lunge at me for another attack.

A brilliant light emitted from the front of the barrel. The force shoved the shotgun back into my gut, leaving me breathless—ironically gasping for life.

In front of me, the little girl stood dazed. Pieces of flesh and bone hung from her frail little face. She was only alive thanks to the activeskin. Her shock was expressed solely through a series of vacant coughs. It was hard to imagine if she had the capacity to fully understand what was happening at that very moment. Hard to imagine any of us did.

She stared into my eyes. Soft and hazel, she used to be the stock photo found in picture frames at department stores. What was left of her light brown hair shimmered in sun rays peaking between houses. It created a stark contrast with hair that was bloodstained and littered with fragments of face, skull, and brain.

All my senses went through various forms of dysfunction at the sound of a single battlerifle shot. I could see, but only blurs. I could feel my chest moving rapidly, but couldn't feel my heartbeat. I heard nothing.

In a blink, my sight returned, but her head was now gone, leaving just her body standing in zombie-like stillness. Blood sprayed out of the jagged edges just above her shoulders. It reached across the backyard, across the windowpanes of the patio behind me, and across my face. Her hands, unmoving; battlebraces remained in attack form.

There is nothing that can prepare you for a headless nine-year-old killer in a sundress. I sat in horror, happy to remain deaf, but momentarily cursed with the return of sight.

Footsteps and a muffled voice finally broke the silence.

"Hey, what happened?" Drake asked as he finally got to my side, observing both his marksmanship and me at the same time.

"I'm sorry, what?"

"What h-a-p-p-e-n-e-d?" Drake repeated.

"I ah, we um…we got back here. She cut me off—"

Drake's eyes never drifted from mine. A type of anger was present in them that was absolutely alien to me. He may very well have been born without a soul. The question is why did he feel the need to see this journey through with me, and not alone?

"Fatty!" Drake yelled, suddenly breaking the silence.

"Yeah?" Lenny's faint voice whined in the distance.

"Get your fat ass out from around the back of that house and find us a car. We're getting the fuck out of here."

C H . 2 0
BIGGER PROBLEMS THAN A LITTLE GIRL

Drake was ahead of me. His pace was more one of purpose, less about self-reflection, like mine.

"Drake?" I started.

"What?"

"Did it strike you odd that a little girl fired a devastational cube with one hand?" I asked, catching up to him. "I mean, it's a fucking rocket launcher, and she just fired it like it was a goddamn Super Soaker."

"No. Why should it?" he shot back, disdain echoing in the silence.

"Do you think you can look past your fucking mood and recognize that a little eighty-pound girl just shot basically a rocket launcher with one arm whilst standing in place? Never mind the fact that we have no idea where she came from."

"Nope."

"Okay. What about the absence of her name on our navguide?"

"What?" Drake fired back. It was obvious that deep thought and the questions it birthed annoyed him.

"Her name. Mr. Polite said—"

"Fuck Mr. Polite."

"Do I need to ban drug use?" I asked. "Have you finally made yourself retarded? Her name didn't come up."

"So? Maybe she was too far away," Drake replied.

"Dick, she was down the street. Not even fifty yards."

"Maybe it malfunctioned."

"Maybe you malfunctioned."

"Fuck you."

The air suddenly held an unfamiliar sound—bits and pieces of scattered chatter spoken through static. Faint at first, it grew louder with each passing second.

"Wait," I said, pausing with my arm outstretched to stop Drake from moving forward. "You hear that?"

Lenny came flying through the other side of the house, crashing through the thin-paneled walls and into the front grill of a pickup in the driveway. Anguish riddled his multilayered face.

Following him was death personified—five people covered completely in black. Their eyes were shrouded in dual ocular lenses. Their bodies rippled with lean muscle, like they had been shrink-wrapped in those uniforms. They brandished the same weapons we held.

Staring at them, the recent events began to play back in my mind in reverse and in slow motion. I saw the little pigtail assassin standing before me once again with half her face off. I remembered why my pause was so prevalent in nature, how my curiosity was awoken and driven to the brink of insanity by the discovery of three shadows. Now it was clear that was not a product of shock or drug relapse. Taking it a step further, maybe this was a clue into why her name was absent from the navguide.

What appeared to be the leader stepped forward, placing himself a foot in front of his men and us. His head cocked to one side, then the other, as if he were reading something. His men waited motionless behind him. I could feel Drake growing more and more uneasy. The sound of his hand tightening the grip on his battlerifle reached my ear. At that moment, I knew he wasn't going to wait for words.

Drake raised his battlerifle and fired at the leader's head. That head snapped back, slamming against the top of his spine. Heat from the rifle burned on the side of my face. Not waiting to see if he killed the leader, Drake opened fire on the rest of the group, sending them scattering back into the hole they created.

"Salt, finish him!" Drake hollered as he dashed behind the pickup for the illusion of cover.

The thought of killing someone was a hard concept to grasp. Even being involved in the previous battles, even almost taking the action myself, to actually take someone's life was nauseating. Worse was the feeling of not having any control over my decision to do so.

This is my life now, I thought.

Raising my weapon, I brought the muzzle up to the leader's head, which was recovering from the point-blank shot. The shimmer that glossed over him confirmed the nightmare my mind had already been loosely exploring—these assholes were protected by activeskin, as we were.

A sudden surge of pain brought me back to reality, and the pull of my trigger was wasted as my round only found the sky. The foot of one of the shadow-figures connected with my hand. He followed with several precise punches to my midsection.

I bent over from the rush of pain, only to have my jaw kicked, sending me back-first onto the pavement. My jaw was having a shit-tastic day.

Now fully recovered, the leader and his minion came at me. Their arms began to glow around the wrist, yielding a familiar hiss. In an instant, both wielded long, katana-like energy blades.

Behind me, Drake continued to use suppressing fire over my position with his battlerifle. One by one, the others tried to join, but recoiled behind cover.

Lenny, of course, was nowhere to be found.

"Fatty! Get your ass out here!" Drake commanded at the top of his lungs.

"Fuck you!" Lenny screamed from behind the house—seemingly his favorite place of refuge, even though that's where he was hit the last time.

Finally getting the clear shot he needed, Drake began taking control with the BSR. Held expertly in his hands, it hollowed smooth chaos in only five shots. One after the other, he killed every last one of them.

"What the fuck?" I screamed over to Drake. My voice was shaken from this last brush with death, some of which was Drake's sniper rounds barely missing my head.

"Is that all five?" Drake asked while approaching the bodies and myself.

"I don't know. I think so."

"Fat boy dead?" Drake asked nonchalantly.

"No," Lenny's meager voice answered as he cautiously came from around the back of the house.

"Next time, aim or keep your fat ass out of sight," Drake coldly instructed.

"What the hell just happened?" I asked. My nerves were still on edge from the past few moments. The battle was only seconds long, I reminded myself. But it didn't matter. It felt like I had just spent a lifetime fighting.

"No clue," Drake answered. His eyes never left the bodies.

"Christ! Lenny what happened behind the house?" I asked.

"Ummm…" Lenny stuttered. "They…they just came out of nowhere. I was walking back to meet you guys around front, when I felt a breeze behind me like something was moving. The next thing I know, I'm on the other side of the house and there's a big fucking hole in front of me, with five homicidal fucking bugmen standing in the space." Lenny's hands were waving all about, frantically trying to match the pace of speech and his heartrate.

"What the fuck…. First, we get junior femme-fataled, and now…?" I asked desperately.

"We have bigger problems than that," Drake blurted.

"Oh yeah? Bigger problems than random uniformed badasses showing up out of left field?" I challenged.

Drake pushed a body with his foot. "These fuckers were military trained."

"How the fuck could you tell something like that?"

Ignoring my frantic question, Drake bent over to grab a battlerifle clutched in one of the dead bugmen's hands. He then handed it to me.

"Let me show you how to hold a rifle."

C H . 2 1
REMEMBER HER LOVE, VERONA

New Mexico, 2007

"Her name was Verona," Sunday interrupted.

"What's that now?"

It was hard enough to keep a steady stream of thought around her as it was. Periodically interrupting me with random jewels of wisdom was making it fucking impossible.

"The little girl. The one that almost killed you? Her name was Verona."

"You knew her?"

"Yes."

"How?"

"I overheard the Alt talking about her before I killed them."

"You heard the Alt?"

"Yes."

I started for the door. Witch portal or not, she could follow me to hell, because I was done with this conversation. I wanted everything—the Battles, this conversation, everything—done. I needed to go kill or get killed.

"Wait, wait, wait. Hold on there, tiger. Don't get all PMSy on me, like some moody teen," Sunday halfheartedly pleaded.

"Come on. It's taking a lot of work to keep this conversation going."

"Nothing you say makes sense to me."

"Just relax. What's the hurry?"

"The Alt don't fucking talk!" I hollered in frustration.

I never once heard them speak to one another. I knew they communicated, being they moved as one, but not once had I ever heard them even grunt. Oh, but of course Sunday hears them.

Sunday was recovering from leaning back from my yell. "Okay, dirty strip club bathroom toothbrush or not, wise choice. But you're not done, sparky. Hit up those gums."

"Why won't you just kill or fuck me?"

"In that order?"

"It's the only way I'd survive, as far as I see it."

"Okay, you're right. They don't actually talk," Sunday continued, ignoring the newest subject of conversation. "And what I heard wasn't actually words."

"You just won't stop until I mentally snap, will you? I'm in hell already, aren't I?"

"Not that lucky. Moving on. Like I told you before, some of us heroes had a faster start to becoming more than the Employers could handle. My path had me hunting the Alt by the time you finally stumbled your way out of Massachusetts."

"Fine," I said, choosing to no longer fight it. It couldn't be any more surprising than my past year. "Why were they hunting little Miss Verona?"

"Because she was just like me, but worse. Keep talking, sweetheart."

C H . 2 2
WHAT PAVLOV'S DOG EXPERIMENT WOULD HAVE RESEMBLED IF FUNDED BY SATAN

Connecticut, 2006

"Keep the butt of the gun—or stock, if you will—up against your shoulder. The recoil will cause your arm to rise if you hold the rifle out in the open like in the movies. You do that, and you won't hit shit. You keep it against your shoulder, hold steady, and breathe calmly, you'll hit your target."

The words echoed through my mind like the sporadic claps of thunder from our weapon discharges. We were standing somewhere outside of Massachusetts, just inside the border of Connecticut that also touches the edge of New York. Taking a detour in the selfish, desperate hope of finding another abandoned police evidence room, and perhaps more weapons caches, we were brought to a tour sponsored by hell.

The town that harbored the exit we chose at random mirrored Hiroshima, August 7, 1945—decimated, with a fresh glow to highlight the obliteration. Although there was really no way of knowing for sure, it was obvious this was a site of severe and swift response to the presence of us subjects.

The houses looked like empty husks of what they used to be, like some monster had feasted on their insides. The streets were blackened with soot and blood. Even the sky held a gray tint, unable to do away with the careless atrocities that transpired days or weeks before. This graveyard neighborhood held remnants of the poor soldiers sent to stop whatever battle had taken place here. Discarded helmets and hollowed-out tanks. Transports and light armor units left to the side, crashed into whatever stopped them from rolling. Sadly, within this massacre, the innocent weren't separated from the intended targets.

Forgetting the intended purpose of our detour, Drake had stopped the car abruptly as we continued on our path to the unknown. It was his firm belief that we didn't know shit about firing a weapon, and were, for the most part, lucky. If we were to proceed, we were in desperate need of some weapons training. Even Lenny.

With a flair for the dramatic (a hidden trait of the sociopath I now call my only friend), Drake dragged us to a choice location and set up a makeshift weapons training course. Scarecrows made of bottles and materials dragged out of abandoned houses were designated as enemies and placed at varying distances throughout the abandoned suburban farmhouse.

It was Drake's understanding that our real targets would be far from predictable and conveniently sized; therefore, setting up variably-sized targets was a necessary step toward making his knowledge fully "pertinent." Large targets were to simulate close quarters. Bottles, cans, dead rats—anything small that could blend in with the background—were set up to simulate targets in the distance. I could only imagine what sniper training would entail.

"Fatty...seriously, what are you shooting at?" Drake said, pacing behind Lenny as he was attempting to hit a target at the far end of the range. Arms behind his back and chin held to the sky in confidence, Drake was as I expect Patton would have been, sans the fat, codeine-laced blunt hanging from between his lips and teeth. A permanent haze happily hung around his face, casting an inhuman shadow.

"I—I...." Lenny choked up.

I didn't think Lenny was ever going to be okay with all of this. Sometimes, the fantasy that lives in your head is supposed to stay there.

"You're fucking wasting ammo," Drake sharply insisted. "You can't hit that. First, the point of having the butt of the weapon up against your shoulder is to help you aim. But, that only works if you have some aim. Second, you, who have the worst eyesight I've seen in quite some time, are trying to hit a bottle over fifty meters away. Unless we find an eye doctor sympathetic to our plight, you are no longer allowed to fire at far targets."

"That's bullshit," Lenny protested.

"Get used to your automatics and shotguns. You're now a close-range soldier. You'll be point on structure entries, and will be responsible for the management of extra supplies."

"So I'm the fucking mule."

"For a lack of a better expression, yes."

"Fuck that. Who says you get to delegate whose roles are whose? Salt, you—"

The words were coldly cut off from a single sidearm round. Hand outstretched and in position to continue firing on his target, Drake stared at Lenny. His eyes were vacant of any emotion, his features highlighted by the end of his blunt, fighting against the contrast of the impending darkness from sunset and rumored government-sponsored post-apocalyptic clouds. Lenny's face, however, was the picture of unabashed fear.

"I could be losing my fucking mind, but I could have sworn I've told you before what your position is in this little club we have here," Drake said. "You see, as chaotic as my mind may seem, it needs solace and structure, and part of that is the fact that I own you." Drake jabbed his gun into Lenny's chest and stomach. "Me. Get it? I own you. And until I kill you, you do what the fuck I say."

The gun wavered in Lenny's face. His face was drenched from sweat, tears, and mucus. I could only look on as one does when they see the beginning of a car crash.

"Very good. Get used to your battlebraces, too," Drake added as he returned the sidearm to the back of his pants. "It's proving to be very useful. Put that big brain to use and wreak havoc." He slapped Lenny on the shoulder. This may have been the most work done toward making Lenny a man in his entire life.

Something caught Lenny's attention through his sobs and bouts of hyperventilation. Considering that he had just received the pep talk of his life, we shouldn't have been surprised to see him forgo telling us what he was going to do and just going ahead and recklessly doing it. Extending both battlebraces, Lenny let out his version of a war cry and charged towards the second house from the end of the street.

"Should we be concerned he just charged forward without saying why or where?" I asked casually.

Drake continued to watch Lenny run toward the house. He took another drag of his blunt and savored watching the moment Lenny realized the house was further away than his adrenaline was able to carry his sprint, and struggled to keep up a steady jog seconds in.

"No."

"Seriously? We don't even want to know why he just took off?"

"Nope."

Lenny was finally in the house and out of sight when he heard him scream.

"Fine," Drake huffed.

C H . 2 3
ALL THE BEST
CHEST MOVES
IVOLVE A HAMMER

"I see you have the three-piece," I said, casually pointing toward BountyLesManly's setup on his bedroom bureau.

Lenny was in the corner of BountyLesManly's bedroom, shitting himself and screaming bloody murder, because it appeared his activeskin wasn't quite working yet. Lenny must've seen BountyLesManly walking into his home and taken it upon himself to attack him.

What was problematic was the fact that we were standing in a hero's room, admiring his devotion to such a devilishly simple, yet near-impossible practice of self-maintenance perched gloriously on his cherry-wood dresser. A dresser in a room belonging to a house the Employers promised to have destroyed.

"So you know of the practice?" BountyLesManly whispered with an appreciative glee, hands clasped together in a respectful steeple.

"Yeah. Tried many times, only to feel the glimpse of certainty in my thought process before fucking leaving some mail on there or some shit."

"Ahhh, always the mail. Horrible aspect of society, don't you think?" BountyLesManly hissed.

"How long have you kept this up? Without fucking it up, I mean."

"Ah, what are you Marys talking about?" Drake groaned. His arms hung limply over the edges of his battleshotgun, which lay across the back of his neck. He despised wasting time before the kill.

"Three years," the man said proudly.

His room felt liked it belonged to a twelve-year-old, but it still had the smell of freshly dead skin and lotion. Might be top five on my list of most disgusting smells. Strong and subtle; the impossible funk. Squished in between his Circle Prophecy videogame "maps" and free pinup posters of videogame vixens was his BS in engineering.

"Three years?" I asked with shock. I was truly impressed, if only for a fleeting moment.

"Three years," he replied. "It is my temple."

"You got to be fucking shitting me..." Drake groaned again.

"Impressive. How so long?" I asked, ignoring Drake.

"As I said..." BountyLesManly began to hiss. His overbite gave way to a protruding, reptilian mouth region. "It is my temple. I wake and sleep with my first and last thought being only three objects on my dresser: my lamp, my molten steel Samus statue—"

"Doll," Drake interrupted while staring BountyLesManly directly in the eyes. He'd had enough of this.

BountyLesManly never turned away. Almost everyone looks away when a homicidal psychopath stares him or her dead in the eye—almost everyone. More and more, I felt that being in his room meant something was wrong, and it was about to get worse.

"And my alarm clock," BountyLesManly continued. "Neither mail nor money nor keys nor phone shall see morning from night on this dresser. And the result, the reward: I have unequivocally focused my thought process into an awesome mental consciousness. I have, in order, answered all but two of the most important questions in my life."

"Any of those questions involve the Employers?" I asked.

"The most important questions in my life occurred before the Battles. Thanks to that, I was able to see clarity once the Battles began."

"Did you see your abduction?"

"I wasn't abducted."

"You expect me to believe that?"

"Look around you. Look at the pictures of people. This is my room. This is my house. Tell me, how is your house?"

The words went past my brain and directly at my soul. Killing him was always a part of the plan if we wanted to survive what the Employers were putting us through, but his adding insult to injury was only going to make it easier. That said, I still needed answers. Mentally wiping the verbal spit from my face, I pressed on.

"Fine, you weren't abducted. How'd you get those?" I said, pointing to his battlebraces.

"So bored…" Drake groaned.

"Relax, Hellokilla. They came to me as they did you. The difference is I went willingly. That fact that you call it an abduction says you did otherwise," BountyLesManly explained.

"Why did you go with them?

"The key to asking the right questions to the meaning of your life is knowing what the answers are."

"One of your three questions?"

"One of my answers was to let go."

"Is this where the bullshit gets thick?" Drake chimed in. His boredom at this point was palpable.

"I didn't ask for nor need your approval in my self-discovery," BountyLesManly snapped.

"Fuck you," Drake launched. "You're the one on a show and tell. You ooze of a childhood full of false confidence, doctored up and administered by a slightly-pedophilic overbearing mother whispering how special you were while you ran through your version of the day after school, fact never necessary to correlate to your points. Just little Bobby's way."

"Fuck you. My name is Derrik, and my mother was a crack whore. It was wonderboy's inquiry into a practice that is obviously above both of you, so to reiterate, fuck you. Do you want me to continue, or should we just fucking do this?"

"That's what the fuck I'm talking about!" Drake howled.

"Wait, wait!" I pleaded.

"Fuck that, hero!" Drake hollered. "There has been far too much time passed between meeting this fucking cock-smoker and killing him. We're heroes, goddammit! Get it together!"

"Cock-smoker? For that, I'll put one in your ass," BountyLesManly retaliated.

"Draw your gun, man!" Drake yelled to the side of my face as I held him back.

"Fucking hold up!"

"What? I should fucking end you next."

"Then do it."

I didn't know why, but there was nothing about what BountyLesManly said that made me want to scream bullshit. I had a pit in my stomach that grew with his every word. I had a sense of finally stumbling onto some clues about what was happening to us—to the world.

"Argh!" Drake screamed.

The room spun. For an instant, my stomach touched my throat, leaving me with sudden nausea. Something very wrong was happening.

I looked down just in time to catch BountyLesManly's hand withdrawing from Drake's abdomen, deliberately slow. His face was painted with a marriage of hatred and pleasure, devoid of remorse or fear.

It appeared that BountyLesManly had been simply plotting his move. He was smart enough to understand a demeanor like Drake's. He knew enough from Drake's first few comments that obvious stereotypical homosexual mannerism would back any swinging dick (Drake) into a state of blind homophobic aggression. And I was slowly beginning to understand that the best-trained killers knew not to attack in aggression.

But fate serves no one that waits. Confidence can lead one to overestimate. Confidence in a flawless tactic can still be the end for those who don't consider every scenario.

BountyLesManly had obviously not considered when stabbing a complete sociopath who can only operate in shades of hate, waiting will get you killed. In a reversal that must have felt like the magnetic poles inverting, BountyLesManly's body flew back toward the wall, shattering a bookcase. Little gray space marine figurines flew everywhere.

Recovering and wincing, but strong enough to rise, Lenny slowly got up, holding the smoking battleshotgun. He didn't wait for our approval and pumped three more rounds into BountyLesManly, until it was pretty clear he was dead.

"Tell me why you let that little fuck stab me!" Drake demanded as he stood to a painful upright.

The damage from the battlebraces was beginning to heal, but not before I could see the exposed side of his stomach through his tattered shirt. Only an inch to the right would have proven fatal, though most mortals wouldn't be standing ready to battle after being stabbed.

"Fuck you if you think I should be sorry," I replied.

"What? You let him stab me!"

"You let him stab you. When the fuck was I egging him into battle? When? Last I fucking checked, I was the one talking to him in a non-hostile tone. A conversation, if you are even fucking familiar with the term."

"This is what we do, Salt. We're heroes. We kill. We got placed in this fucked position only to kill. It's not going to end until we kill everyone, then each other."

"Where are we? We're in his fucking room, Drake. That's not strange to you? Our houses were skate parks when we got to them, and this weird fuck was chilling in his room. His room, you fucking child, his room! Are you the asshole on the main deck not seeing the Titanic sinking as lawn chairs fucking fly past you? Fuck it, I'm off this. Chubby!"

C H . 2 4
MISSING THE TREE
FALLING ON YOU
IN THE FOREST

New Mexico, 2007

"What bothered you the most during all that?" Sunday asked, cutting into my storytelling. Surprising, because I was convinced I had lost her about halfway through the story.

"Gonna have to go with the fact that we were standing in that asshole's house. Which was weird, because we were under the strange impression that every hero's existence was wiped the fuck out. You get that feeling when the area around where your home used to be looks like a shitty bootleg skate park."

"Is that what you think happened?"

"Should I not?"

"Doesn't matter. So, being in the hero's house was the most unsettling aspect of that battle?"

"Well, the mastery of the three-piece bureau set was a little hard to swallow. I mean—"

"I need you to concentrate."

"Well, what the fuck? I don't know what you want! Shit, I don't even know why you keep visiting me, if I disgust you so much. Either tell me what you want, kill me, or let me finish brushing my teeth and go back out there and enjoy some titties before Drake finally goes psychopath and we have to leave this place."

"You are a bitch, I'll give you that. And yes, there are times I feel like I could be doing a thousand things more productive than listening to you piss and moan. But Samytus thinks you are of value, so here we are."

"Fuck you, fuck Samytus, and fuck everyone else involved in this godforsaken orgy of senseless violence. I didn't ask to be a part of this. I didn't ask to have my loved ones and acquaintances killed. I didn't ask to become a killer!"

"Take it down a notch, sugertits."

"And now you're insulting me with Drake's pet names."

"Full confession: I am addicted to that one. I've been calling everyone sugertits."

"I hate you."

"Of course you do, sugartits. Anyway, focus. What didn't you see?"

"Seriously? This conversation is really making me feel like brushing my teeth with this random toothbrush was my best decision today."

Sunday disgustingly glanced at the toothbrush in my hand. The life of the hero these days were woefully bereft of creature comforts, sure, but most did not have to subject themselves to the level of depravity I was currently relishing with a touch of judgment.

"It's not," she answered plainly. "How many battles had you been in up to that point?"

"I don't know. Maybe ten or so."

"Ten, or more?"

"More."

"How many?"

"You can continue to ask me, but unless you have a trick to read my mind, then fuck off. I don't remember exactly."

"But more than ten?"

"Yes."

"How many times did the Alt show up during or after a battle?"

"Most of them."

Sunday shook her head. "How can anyone be this good and be this aloof?"

"Just fucking lucky, I guess."

"Did it bother you that the Alt didn't show up for that battle?"

"No."

"No? Why not?"

"Didn't give a shit. Why the fuck would I care? Less work for me."

"Even with the questions in your head about how abnormal the situation was, you still didn't care that the Alt didn't bother to show up to investigate?"

"No."

"Why? When did the Alt show up when you battled?"

"It felt random, so that's why I didn't bother to care to remember. Didn't seem necessary. Why do you care?"

"The easiest way to hunt a hero is to follow the Alt. That's how I knew about that little girl that kicked your ass before getting blindsided by your better half."

"First, that little monster was stronger than she looked. Second, not my fault she didn't have a crew. Maybe if she were nicer, she would've had someone watching her back. Fuck her. Next life, have your head on a swivel."

"Remarkably petty."

"You'd feel the same if you fought her."

"More to the point, the Alt lost contact with that hero you were just speaking of. How'd you two find him?"

"We weren't looking for him. Like I said, we were there for target practice. Lenny saw something, decided to show us he's a man, and charged after it."

"So it's Lenny…" Sunday said, seemingly to herself.

"What's that now?"

"You two were following Lenny."

"Hi, I'm Salt. The psycho I call a partner out there is Drake. Have you listened to anything I have said?"

"He got you and Drake together. He caused you to stop and face the first aberration in the Employers' system with that powerful little girl hero. Then, battles later, it was Lenny who found the hero the Alt could not. It was because of him you were able to witness another abnormality that continued to push you past the limits set in front of you by the new realities established by the Employers. If it wasn't for Lenny, the two of you would probably be dead."

"Yeah, well, relax. There were plenty of Alt hunting us and other heroes moving forward."

"Whose idea was it to go west?"

"It's west!" I said, throwing my hands up. The answer felt logical on its face. Why not go west? We started on the East Coast. Going east felt restricting. If not, there'd be a lot of swimming.

So what if Lenny might have said it?

C H . 2 5
WAS THAT BULLET MEANT TO KILL US OR INVITE US?

New York, 2006

The day started off as per usual: a splitting headache and spotty memories of murderous thoughts or unknown events. Mentally lost while standing in some bombed-out tenements, I was well into an internal rant, amazed at our journey being able to continue on highways.

Not sure why we chose Brooklyn to stop and look around. Maybe Drake thought he could score more drugs.

All the buildings were gutted, giant, upright exoskeletons of cockroaches. Everything was painted with a post-apocalyptic brush; the only color discernable from the shades of gray were swatches of red from recent blood and remnants of what was once off-white, tan, or gray walls of the buildings littering the streets, along with the bodies that had yet to be claimed. Little to claim when there is barely more than ashes.

"What are we doing here?" Lenny asked through his wheezing. He was prone to do that after strenuous activity, like walking or getting out of the car.

Following his words was a bullet. It struck the wall directly behind me at head level. The next second brought a rainstorm of bullets.

"You got to be shitting me. Salt, you see where he was?" Drake yelled over the increased gunfire.

Concrete and dust flew up from the missed shots. We walked right into this.

"There's nothing on the navguide!" Lenny yelled.

Directly in front of us was one of the bombed-out high-rises. It looked like it was hit with a missile. The building was missing an entire section, reaching from about the third floor to damn near the top. Each floor remained eerily intact (save the portion blown back to the Ice Age), with all its contents remaining—albeit ashen images of their former selves.

Beginning at the ground floor was a tunnel that descended into the darkness beneath the building. It looked as if it was created by another blast, but this one opened into an underground cavern. Sharing the same reaction as Drake, I took off toward the entrance.

I was about to enter the cavern when I ran into Drake's cautionary hand.

"Be easy, Salt," he said. "You just learned how to hold a gun. This is all still pretty much new to you." His eyes searched mine, judging my resolve in the same manner he did in North Andover.

"Fatty, you're on guard," Drake commanded.

"Fuck you," Lenny replied.

His self-gratification was cut short by a round dissolving into his activeskin. Drake's arm once again stretched out in dramatic fashion, expressing his disdain for Lenny talking back.

"I tell you Lenny, I'm not so good at this whole repeating thing, so let's just assume that the next time will be the last time. Make sure our asses are covered. We'll be back. Stay alive. You don't have the right to die yet." Drake grinned through the gun's smoky discharge.

His words held an uncanny doomsday assurance. He turned

back towards the entrance after feeling satisfied in his final warning.

The passage ran deep beneath the surface. It turned out the building ran directly into an access tunnel that connected the entire grid of this side of the borough—an entire cavern of intertwining tunnels and holes. The flash fire from the blast above found its way inside from any open hole and burned so incredibly hot that the paint had peeled off the walls, then instantly hardened, leaving a coral-like surface.

From deeper within the dark of the tunnels came noise. A rapid beat. It was clear that it was house music, but with a slower, steadier rhythm, more paced and deliberate. Blown-out speakers gave a creepy air to the sound, like it was twice-filtered.

I looked at Drake, confused.

He just shrugged and replied, "That's what I fucking love about New York. No matter what, NYC will always have a club."

C H . 2 6
EVEN THE DANCEHALL GENERAL

Sure as shit, at the end of the dingy tunnel was a dugout. An entire underground chamber. Holed walls bore windows into the next section of the chamber. And within all of this, thousands of people in the midst of lawless rejoice.

One deep breath brought me to an entirely new dimensional plane, whether voluntary or not. Toxic fumes controlled the ratio to clean air. The acidic smell of puke in the abandoned corners of the chamber didn't help, either.

The crowd was all lulled to a zombie-like state thanks to their drug of preference. The room seemed to sway with unified movement of the side-to-side of the masses following the melodic barking of the dancehall general standing next to the DJ in alcove overlooking the crowd..

The DJ hypnotically worked the turntables while the dance-hall general in Jamaican military fatigues and a Nat Turner beard commanded in broken patwa to his disciples of the night. When he spoke, his voice was muffled and distorted, but the crowd understood him well, as if he actually connected with each of them subconsciously with every word.

"Drake…we're fucked."

The words left my mouth in a trance. The roomed slowed to a crawl. Every motion and movement around me all but stopped and traced over itself. Every color in the room blended together, then burned itself as shadows across my retinas.

Suddenly, everyone turned their zombie attention toward us with lifeless eyes. They were waiting, and as painful seconds passed, it felt like they were waiting for us. The music didn't skip a beat. I didn't even feel Drake's hands shake me.

"He—hhhheeeyyy...hey!" Drake shouted as he tried to shake me back to reality. "You're fucking high!"

"What?" The words felt like molasses spilling from my mouth.

"Yooouu'rrreee high. This air, it's all tainted. Look over there." He pointed to the corners of the chamber. "Those are fucking acid meth inhibitors. It's basically vaporizing meth crystals into the room's atmosphere. These peoples are just junkies."

"Wait, wait.... Why do you know all this? Why aren't you fucked up?" I stumbled to ask.

"Shit, son, this is my cappuccino on a rainy day. As for the knowledge, any rave worth the sweat off a pink-haired pixie has at least one going for the crowd. You didn't really believe the 'I just go for the dancing' bit, did you?"

"Ummm...no," I said, attempting to apply my index and middle fingers to my temples, failing to gain control of my brain. My voice became comically deep. The words were said before I had time to process them.

"Good. Now, you have to snap out of it."

"I'm really fucked up."

"I know. The world has slowed to a crawl, hasn't it?" Drake asked. There was an unfamiliar but comforting reassurance in is voice.

I could feel my head slowly nodding an answer, but in my mind, I was already two sentences ahead. "I think my teeth are bleeding?"

I reached into my mouth.

"Do not do that," Drake said calmly as he grabbed my wrist.

"A, we are in the bowels of a Section 8 high-rise. Putting your unwashed finger in your mouth will kill you faster than any battle could. And B, you may make the high you are experiencing worse."

"Huh? How could that make my high any worse? It's in the air."

My grip on my mental faculties was slipping by the second, like schizophrenia on the clock. Ironically, the more I had to breathe, the more ground I lost.

"Anything that vaporizes will produce a form of condensation. In this case, residue covers the entire place, leaving party favors on virtually everyone and everything. We are standing in the middle of it. You putting your finger into your mouth with such little exposure to this type of high will send you into a comatose state."

"So why aren't you catatonic?" I asked—or at least, my mind believed I asked.

"Like I said, my cappuccino on a rainy day," Drake replied with a wink. It felt wrong to find solace in the devil's smile. "I know this is going to sound impossible, but you have to get a hold of this."

I closed my eyes. Though everything remained in slow motion, the room swaying from side to side was beginning to take its toll. Against the hot rush that takes over from this sort of chemical high, a strong feeling of nausea was also setting in. My stomach turned violently, threatening at every second to projectile vomit on everything around me.

"How?" I muttered.

"What?"

"How the fuck do I get a hold of—" I paused to fight back the vomit, then it hit me.

It wasn't some faith-shaking epiphany on how to overcome potent illicit drugs, but a bullet. Single and intentional, the impact squarely on my forehead. In that one second, a new kind of reality took over.

The room remained two steps behind my working perception of the present, but now the lethargic body reactions were missing. That mysterious bullet opened up a whole new world in which I now existed moments into the future.

The bullet was fired from across the room. Standing unapologetically on stairs that looked to be ascending somewhere else was a lone figure. The light bearing down from behind him cast a shadow around his entire body, making it impossible to make out any details.

"You've ventured too far. This is where your stories end," the man announced in an unnecessarily dramatic fashion.

"You've got to be shitting me," I muttered.

"The world abhors the likes of you. It will purge your evil kind from its surface, as it has all parasites from before."

"Blah, blah, blah. I'm a big, drugged-out fuck-nut. I get it! Anything else, or can we be done with this already?" Drake yelled.

"Ah, excellent. In your inability to express yourself vociferously, you presume carnage will conclude the matter. An even greater postulation of illogical faith in the minutely plausible chance of survival," quipped the man.

The tone and pitch in his voice begged one to think of him as some evil jester hell-bent on destruction, similar to Batman's Joker, but more maniacal. It didn't help that we couldn't see him thanks to the blinding light flooding in from behind.

In that second, it was painfully clear how much shit we had stepped in. All the zombified people in the chamber disrobed and brandished hero weapons.

"What the fuck?" Drake whispered. He began to circle around me to determine our situation, careful not to upset the crowd. "We're fucked," was the only thing he could come up with.

"I behoove you to appreciate that amongst this throng of volunteered automatons of the toxic persuasion, most welcomed guest, are those armed with the very same weapons you wield so gallantly. Though they are but mere mortals instruments, pain is a feeling they've parted with long ago. Thus, their pain-driven conception of the afterlife has grown truant from their consciousness, revealing in its wake the most ruthless of killers. You do not scare them, nor do your abilities amaze them. They will fight until they are all departed from this plane of existence, or until you are. God be with you, for he holds no court here."

The man calmly turned and disappeared into the light as he walked up the stairs.

Even though I tried with every fiber of my being to fight the effects of the evaporated drugs, I still fell to illusions. As soon as the mysterious man finished speaking, I could've sworn two mountains dressed in suits came from behind and escorted him out of the chamber. The man's promise of doom wasn't helping the hallucinations.

"This doesn't feel right. Even by killing mob standards." Drake nodded to the crowd that continued to refrain from firing.

"You been in a lot of killing mob situations, Drake?"

"A few."

"I got the worst feeling that they're waiting for a signal."

"Very good, but did you know the signal was us?"

"We have to follow that man."

"Focus, Salt."

Drake's words rolled off me. It wasn't as if I didn't hear him or the words weren't registering, but they were received with the same urgency as the directives of another conversation three tables away in a crowded yuppie restaurant.

I didn't feel my finger tense from contact with the trigger, then tighten into a pull. The first bullet exploded from a burst of blue fire in the nozzle. The thunder came out in a series of thuds, similar to a drumbeat. Time was nonexistent, or just standing still. Bodies frozen in motion.

What was left of the crowd finally returned fire. I had no time to determine their level of innocence in all this, not when their eyes displayed such determination to see me dead over seeing another day. Tomorrow was purely coincidental to them.

Between the two of us, the room went silent in under a

minute. The beat from the turntable needle skipping off debris on the record provided a freakish, empty heartbeat to the chamber. Everyone was dead—even the Dancehall General.

C H . 2 7
TO GOD I SEND YOU

Breaking through the building's rusted steel bulkhead, we were violently exposed to the harsh contrast of the outside. The sunlight triumphantly broke through the grey atmosphere, coming down on us like a wave. The air was cold and crisp.

It hadn't escaped me that we were no longer in Brooklyn, or even a forgotten, bombed-out section of NYC—let alone the rest of the seemingly standard hellhole the country had become. Nothing here was affected. It was as if the Battles never happened. The buildings sparkled in pristine glory. People hurried about, as determined and unapologetic as before. We weren't even given a second look as they brushed past us.

"Can you see him?"

"You do know we're standing in the middle of uptown Manhattan, don't you?" Drake asked casually. "Salt. What the fuck will we gain from chasing these guys down?"

"Another day. He found us, he toyed with us, and he almost killed us. I have no timetable, and generally, no direction. So since we generally have no fucking plan to adhere to, do you think it be alright if I occasionally want to know more about some freak showing up to a reggae rave and commanding them all to kill us? Oh, and if that's cool, I'd also like to find out more about the ability to up and fucking arm people out of nowhere. If that's cool?"

"Still waiting for your point. So far, I've heard this unknown charge for heroics and no real answers. As if some half-a-fag with meth mist machines and a DJ is any more of a threat than any other like us. We are in the shit, my friend. It's all fucked."

"Big difference between facing off with an equal and facing an individual who wields an obscene amount of power just to kill us. I'm going after them."

"Still don't get your point."

"So, does it bother you that there was no mention of controlling people as an ability by Polite?"

"Nope."

"Why?"

"Cause fuck Polite, that's why."

"Fine, but does it fucking even tickle your goddamn fancy that we went from a bombed-out warzone once known as Brooklyn Heights to a well-populated and seemingly unaffected Manhattan—which, by the way, looks as if the Battles have never fucking happened?"

"First," Drake said, "we walked the tunnels for at least an hour with no map, so yeah, I can see us ending up in a new borough. Second, Bloomberg."

"You got to be shitting me."

"Look, I fucking lived here off and on for the last ten years. That fucker keeps shit clean. Money moves mountains."

"How much of this do you believe?"

Suddenly, the crowd reacted to something down the street as a single organism would avoid danger. A wave of panic rippled down the street, sending people stampeding away.

When we worked our way through the crowd, the trio was raining doom down upon the unsuspecting masses by destroying all the surrounding rooftops. I had no idea why this was important to them. What could they possibly gain from this? Why did this guy want to see us dead? Could this day get any fucking weirder?

Drake moved to the top of one of the parked cars on the

street. On reaching the roof, he took in a deep breath and held. His eyes were so still he looked like a mannequin. The drugs currently ravishing his system from his daily diet added to the gloss of those plastic retinas, but held no effect on his hawkish sight when it came time to kill. They didn't even know Drake was there until the first bullets drilled into their bodies.

Drake took down one of the giants, who fell with an ear-shattering cry. His companions, taking no interest in sharing the fate, broke into a reckless sprint. Drake's bullets traced their steps, some making contact.

Traffic slammed to a deadly stop. Cars flew over the ones in front of them, while buses and trucks jackknifed through the streets, obliterating everything in sight.

"To God I send you!" the suit yelled to the skies. When his head came down from the curse, his eyes were red from broken blood vessels.

The world went black. Emptiness consumed my surroundings. I scratched at my eyes to make sure they weren't forced shut. I called out to Drake to make sure I wasn't dead. His voice was distant, but still there.

Then, everything went white—sharp, like sun glaring off fresh snow. Blinding to pure obscurity. I could not even fathom the range my eyes were going through. The contrast alone sent such strong signals to my brain, they induced a crippling migraine. I fell to my knees to cope with the pain. Every breath I took felt like my last. My mouth opened to release sound, but nothing came out.

An eternity slipped past me before I realized Drake propped me up against one of the overturned, wrecked cars in the middle of the street. God only knew where the fuck Lenny was.

While Drake was doing his soldier-on-drugs routine, a man stood behind him. He was common enough—nothing really out of sort. Probably mid-forties, probably a public lawyer or an accountant or some shit. But he was holding a gun.

Once I noticed that, I also noticed that he wasn't alone. The entire surrounding crowd within a block's radius stood with him. All armed. Before I could say it, the first wave of bullets went sailing by my head.

"You got to be shitting me! Fuck!" I hollered after ducking behind the car Drake had me propped up on. The bullets were making short work of the car, limiting my time and options.

"What the fuck happened?" Drake demanded as he joined me.

He wasted little time on the thought of killing civilians. He didn't arm them, and he didn't tell them to fire.

One by one, like the cans back in the bombed-out town, Drake took them down. He didn't discriminate. Every man, woman, and child holding a weapon got one between the eyes. The scary part—they didn't even attempt to save themselves. They approached with blind intent. It was clear the same thing that happened in the reggae rave chamber was happening again.

"You better fire, man," Drake said, his cool concentration fixed on incoming enemies. He didn't even concern himself with those approaching from the opposite direction—or least, I thought he didn't.

"We're surrounded. I can tell from the impacts to the car and my side. It won't be long before this crowd of 'innocent' people overtake us and kill us. I've already neutralized thirty from this direction, and I'm still killing. Get on your gun and take them down."

The words were cold coming from his mouth. There was no fear, no doubt.

"Fire your weapon, man!" Drake demanded.

Taking up my battlerifle, I rose to rest the barrel on the side of the car. Bullets immediately paraded into my skull as I got lit up. I could feel the world going black again. In that moment, I came closer to death than I ever have. My heart could be heard down the street. The fear crippled me completely.

"Right now, you're only scared," eased Drake.

Understanding the previous course of action was the wrong

one, I sprinted to the other side of the street, to the back of an old-fashioned, all-steel NYC subway entrance. Once behind it, I leaned left to get a better view of the open street.

My mind began to wonder once more into the what was happening and not the moment at hand, but was brought back to the present by a bullet. Opening fire, the powerful kick felt almost soothing. My guilt went with every bullet, my prayers with every dropped body. I existed on an entirely different plane at that moment.

"We got to get out of here."

"You got a better idea?" Drake asked. It's amazing how clearly I was able to hear him. It was as if we weren't even engaged in a heavy firefight at all.

"I'm running out of ammo, and I know you are, too."

"Got sidearms and the battlebraces," Drake yelled back.

"Fuck you. Listen, you can stay here and kill Peter, Paul, Mary, and the schoolchildren all you want. I'm going after the suit."

"You don't even know where he went."

"Don't think it'll be hard tracking them down."

"Don't too far and make me make you regret this decision."

"Good luck to you, too, Drake."

Taking faith that the zombies didn't have much aim or the strength of activeskin, I took off right toward them. The bullets found both my body and the pavement. The ones that found my body sent the type of pain signal to my brain you'd associate with being pricked with a needle. It was manageable at first, but as I got closer to them, more shots were concentrated, and the pain became more intense, as if the next prick would morph into bullet hole. I could've turned to fire, but I wasn't entirely sure I would've been able to kill all those who had a shot at me before my activeskin gave out.

Finally clear of the main wave of people, I could see that I was right—it wouldn't be hard to track the suit. He and the giant had continued on foot, and the chaos left behind made them easy to track.

Countless disillusioned bystanders wandered the street, still dazed from the mobile mayhem. Surprisingly, the suit and his bodyguard didn't get far. Time was once again playing with my tenuous grip on reality.

With a clear shot in line, I fired at the other giant. The burst of bullets found the back of his head, sending him forward in a silent tumble. The suit stopped. He didn't look shocked. He didn't cower, or even cover. He just stared. He shook his head like he'd made up his mind, and walked toward me.

Not sure if I was experiencing latent effects from the meth from before, but I could have sworn the sky and everything behind him was getting darker. Suddenly, standing and fighting wasn't the grand plan I once envisioned. I knew enough to think shooting at an individual who could alter the brightness of the entire world behind him was perhaps a wasted effort.

Looking around for a quick escape from the walking thunderstorm, I found an unattended and oddly undamaged Fat Boy resting to my right, among the many other motorcycles lined up in front of a swanky little yuppie biker bar.

I took solace in the oversized wheels of the modified euro-rocket, and didn't give a fuck about the owner or breaking any laws. The owner was probably lying in one of the piles Drake, myself, or the lunatic suit created.

The bike roared awake. The ignition was no problem, thanks to the battlebraces. Lights from the dashboard splashed onto my face. It was by far the coolest thing I'd ever been on. My mind raced with situations in which I would even sniff the 250 miles per hour on the gauge. So what if I had absolutely no clue on how to ride it?

Then I could feel my mind starting to warp. It felt like someone was physically bending and twisting my brain like Play-Doh. I looked behind to see the very image that brought me to the bike.

I banged a u-turn, and took off speeding past the suit. There was an unaffected street at the intersection just beyond him. Traffic flashed by as I reached speeds mortals dared not achieve in a crowded city. The cars, buses, trucks, and people were the last things on my mind. That suit? He was turning people into gun-toting zombies with a simple decree. He was running around with those giants like the fucking Riddler and henchmen fleeing a scene. He wanted us dead. Aside from my next move, there really wasn't anything else worth contemplating at the moment.

My attention was violently brought back to the now. A familiar hiss went past my ear. Looking behind, I could see the suit decided to give chase. Riding on a motorbike like me, he masterfully held the handlebars and fired his weapon at the same time.

He then began to affect the world once more. Cars and people were breaking their course with the sole purpose of hitting me. Buses inadvertently pulled away from their routes to block my path or crush me.

The only option I hadn't explored was complete and utter insanity, so I took a sharp left into an open building entrance to a generic New York skyscraper—possibly a bank. The outside walls stretched to the clouds in proud, black marble and steel. The entrance was lined with ten glass doors—enough space to make it through at least one of them. Leveling the glass with one of my sidearms, I sped through to the sound of falling glass, fear, and shock. I didn't know what I was doing. I just knew the suit chasing me trumped every sane option.

My increasingly lunatic mind mused on every new idea of escape that grew grander and crazier. I knew the suit was behind me. I could tell by the screams that suddenly went silent. I somehow found my way to the roof of the building, through incredible navigation of a series of emergency stairwells and wrecked office floors.

The presence of fresh air was always welcome. The roof seemed as long as a football field, but in seconds, I could see the sharp line that separated the roof from the distance below. The closer to the edge I came, the more of the rest of the city—including the next building—was in view.

Even the gunship.

Exposed like a turtle's head came the largest gun turrets I had ever seen on any flying vessel. Long and wide, they gleamed, deceptively playful in the sunlight. The most frightening image of all: within the hull stood multiple Alt, staring back at me.

Caught in the moment, I failed to realize they had already opened fire. In unison, multiple devastational-cube rockets raced past me and at the roof entrance.

I had less than a second to see the suit emerging from the door before the rockets found their target. The impact left nothing, sending shockwaves throughout the building and down to the foundations. Whatever the suit was, he wasn't alive anymore.

Feeling the rush of wind at the heights of a thirty-story building, my attention came back to the hovering gunship filled with Alt. Why did they want the suit dead more than me? Ignoring the indulgence to ponder the questions, I quickly weighed my options.

Cranking the throttle, I launched myself off the roof.

In that moment, when even gravity was catching up with me, I could hear everything. I could hear the unsuspecting people below. I could hear the thunderclap of Drake's rifle back at his position. And I could hear the gears in the ship and the clicks of freshly reloaded weapons on board.

The bike and I parted. Disconnecting brought another rush of cold air over my body. The weight of the bike pulled it faster toward the gunship.

The Alt inside tilted their heads quizzically at the action. Apparent sacrifice must not have been an action they calculated. Power coursed through my body with the emergence of the greenish blue light that hailed a large blade from both of my battlebraces.

As I soared through the air, I brought it back behind my head. Finally close enough, I struck the hovering bike. The blade sliced through effortlessly. A small explosion emitted from the violent separation, sending two uncontrollable objects toward the gunship. The impact sent the ship reeling backward. A blue flame torched the sky as the gunship suffered a series of explosions and disappeared behind the rapidly vanishing cityscape.

Nothing about that moment felt like it was going to be my last.

C H . 2 8
SUNNY DAY
DISPOSITIONS

Pennsylvania

Against the backdrop of a perfect sunlit day, complete with postcard blue skies and vacation inspiring breeze, I sat staring into the abyss of my coffee. Staring into a small pool of jet-black will bring the trance to anyone. The ripples in my cup, emanating from the center to the outer edges, were due to the chaos caused by the drug-fueled hands of my partner in fate, Drake, instructing Lenny through the battle currently raging on outside.

Drake decided that he needed to show Mr. 4lphabody the ropes while I took the backseat and observed alone in the diner. If it weren't for the stench of death, it would have been a scene of pure comedy. All that said, the inside of this rusty diner held the real bedlam.

"Sunny day. Mind if I join you?"

The question came from a kindly old man standing in front of my booth. He had to have been in his eighties. Just a guess, but a solid guess, considering he was dressed to the nines, and I severely doubted he had anywhere to go. His skin, tan despite his age, suggested a lifetime of hard labor against an open field's sun. But underneath his bushy white eyebrows and wise owl's spectacles showed a welcoming face.

"I'm not exactly great company," I responded.

"The booth is open. You're staring blankly at an empty cup of coffee…."

"There's coffee in this cup?"

"You're one of those heroes, aren't you?" he asked with a hint of excitement as he sat down, skipping the invitation's acceptance.

"Be easy. I'm just a man who's—"

"The thing I find interesting about the youth is that you always assume your experience is the first of its kind."

"So tell me, where in this country's history did I miss that even begins to resemble what I, and the rest of us poor fucks, are going through? As far as I know, nowhere. So at least give me the respect that I am in unsettled historical territory, and my experiences, albeit hard to believe, or even understand, are unique and above personal reflective scrutiny."

"Such a tempered soul," the old man whispered while shaking his head.

"Can we skip to the part where you go on about going up a five-mile hill to school in five feet of snow? It's the part I'm actually unfamiliar with."

"I watched you. I've watched your friends," the old man said quietly while rapping his knuckles on the booth's window.

Outside, in the sunlight, among the birds and flowers, Drake and Lenny were still embroiled in battle. Drake had total control of the situation, enough so that he amused himself by toying with Lenny against the rest of the fumbling, battling subjects.

"It's sad," the old man said. "You heroes have walked this country on a dark path."

"What part got you to that deep revelation? That our sole purpose in life now is to kill? Or because despite our best efforts, death follows us, whether we choose to participate or not?"

"No. It's your anger that is sad. It has consumed you to no end. You walk heavy, son. Two shadows, but not in sense of the

Holy Ghost."

I could hear something coming in the distance, but only in my head. The sound started weak, then grew strong and foreboding, like hearing a car off in the distance lose control. It came closer and closer, but instead of bracing for impact, I breathed in deep and complete. A rush from the natural high of oxygen brought me out of my daze and into the present. Naturally confused and struggling with whether or not I was actually asleep, it took looking outside to remember where I was; the pool of drool on the tabletop and the empty seat across from me to realize I had been dreaming.

The dream felt so real. The conversation resonated in my mind like a fresh scolding made sharp by someone respected and painful to disappoint. I could picture his face. Every part of me believed he was just sitting in front of me.

The booth was identical to the dream—high crown with rotted, crimson leather cushions. The tablecloth was a lumber-jack-plaid green. And in keeping with the eerie consistency, my cup was filled with the same abyssal black coffee, though the cup was cold.

Outside was the same demonic playground I had envisioned. Drake and Lenny were engaged in a massive melee. Had to be over twelve subjects out there. The old man in my dream called us heroes.

We are not heroes.

"Sunny day. Mind if I join?" The words trailed back to the wrinkled gentlemen kindly standing before me.

I couldn't help but stare. Every part of me wanted to ask if we had met before. I quickly nodded to the seat across from me.

"You're one of those heroes, aren'tcha?" the old man whistled through his teeth. His eyes were filled with glee.

"What gave it away? The really big gun resting on the table, or the even bigger gun at my side?"

He stared at me for a moment before sitting, as if something new had come to a stale scene.

"Are you high?" he asked.

The question threw me off. Up until this moment, I had thought I was now able to throw off all the visible signs of being high. It was most likely the drugs that brought on that confidence.

"Yes," I answered blankly.

"Goddamn, that's hot! What's that like?" the man asked, smacking his knee with his hat.

"What's what like?" I asked, confused.

"That feeling. That feeling of not giving a fuck. That feeling like you don't give a good goddamn because you could die at any moment."

"Gotta tell you, never really thought of it like that."

"Ahh, come on! You're a hero. I've seen you guys. Fucking mean. I saw one of you fuckers in Tulsa just a few months ago. Scary-looking fuck. Most heroes don't look like much. Like you and me, you know?" He paused to hang his finger in the air, trembling and shaking, wrinkled with the care only a lifetime of hard labor could give.

"Umm...yeah," I mumbled in response.

"But this little fuck looked like pure death," the old man continued. "Pale as the horse the avenging angel rode in on, you know? Dressed in nothing but black. I was in town to get some feed, maybe some bait if I had some time to fish, you know?"

Again, that fucking finger hung, waiting, pointing right through me. For a moment, I could swear I felt the sensation of a bullet passing through my body.

"Well, anyway. He comes walking down Main Street, cars be damned. He didn't once flinch from his course. Just walked perfectly straight down the double yellow lines. Then, all of a sudden, five masked fellas came leaping out of nowhere and just opened up a whole lotta pain on him. For five minutes, nothing but flashes and bangs. They destroyed everything that surrounded the dark fella, except him. The fella removed what looked like a cape that was only covering one side. Well, he unlatched that and drew two pistols. Next thing you know, he was darting all around like a spitfire or lightning bolt. Those masked men didn't know what hit 'em. It was over faster than a flash sandstorm."

"And?" I asked. Not to say I wasn't impressed with the daunting feat of defeating what sounded like five of the Alt; I just sorta felt like there was supposed to be more to the story.

"The fucker just kept walking, as if nothing ever happened."

"Interesting," I muttered, caring less about my inability to hide my sarcasm.

"Just saying, not many people would be able to do something like that. If they could, they sure as shit wouldn't be able to just continue walking on down the street."

"He was probably still in shock."

"In shock from what?" the man asked.

"That he was capable of such a thing."

"It's got to be exciting."

Right when the obvious answer—at least to me—was about to leave my lips, the interaction of skull and diner window distracted our conversation. We could thank a Drake-instructed Lenny for the interrupting thud as he continued to aggressively overcome his opponent with the use of his environment. Drake stood next to him proudly, giving an approving head nod.

"We are not the heroes," I corrected. I couldn't accept it.

"Every story needs a hero, son. And since good and bad is merely perception, to us, you're all we have."

"Why do you want to know what is like to be one of us? Aren't you terrified of this?"

"Son, I've been on the doorstep of death for almost thirty years now. I've worked my entire life for a goal I did not know wasn't even mine until I obtained it. They said you had to go college. I went. They said get a good secure job. I became a farmer. They said save up, buy a house, and start a family. Bought a house, had a wife, saw three kids to college. Go to church. Sit at home and read. Drive the speed limit. Followed the model to a T. Now what? I'm miles away from the only home I've ever known because a battle left my house and farm nothing more than ashes, and the only thing that bothers me is that I've spent my whole life following someone else's plan. I have no wild memories, once-in-a-lifetime events, or things that would pass as even a remotely entertaining story. Sad to think you had eighty-nine years to have a life and you really didn't live it."

"Think you're walking through sunken dreams," I said. "Twenty-twenty hindsight has made you a bit too rough on your personal nostalgia. We all end up on a treaded path."

"Not you heroes."

C H . 2 9
INTROSPECTION IS MEANT FOR THE INTROSPECTIVE

Indiana

"You know, I wasn't always a dick," Drake casually announced.

My response was simply, "I can't imagine."

"I wasn't. Really," Drake pleaded, then shrugged. "Used to be a sweet kid."

"I can't see it."

"It's hard seeing this evil. You think this shit comes naturally to me?

"Ummm...yeah. That's close to what I had in mind."

"I don't just wake up pissing evilness, you know."

"You are a sick fuck," Lenny chimed in, taking opportunity where only he saw fit.

"Shut it, fatty," Drake snapped. "The day your opinion matters...." He held his hand out in aggression, only to shake his head with frustration.

"Something about being a dick takes concentration...?" I prompted.

"See. That wasn't as easy as you think."

"Do you have two brains?" I asked honestly.

"I came to you for a team. A partnership."

"Just so you can be the one to kill me. Noble in theory, but still disconcerting."

"Salt, Salt. You think I'd kill you before it's time? Before our very own historic doomsday showdown, volume one? You think I'd fucking cheat that opportunity?"

"Yes," Lenny said, hoping to add his two cents while the conversation provided cover.

He was soon corrected. The air cracked from a single sidearm round as Drake withdrew his hand from a sneaky position aimed at Lenny's forehead. Lenny held his head from both pain and loss of pride. The smoke flowed devilishly around Drake's face, highlighting gaunt dimensions generally reserved for really fucking deranged individuals.

"So tell me, soul crucified after Christ back from sweet rapture, how did the sword fall into your hand?"

The day had been ungodly boring up until that point. I was hoping the load of bullshit Drake inevitably shoveled back would make it all worth it.

"I gotta tell you, Salt—I like that. I like that a lot. Think I might get that tatted somewhere."

"Can we even get tattoos with this activeskin on?" Lenny asked. He was painfully reminded once more that he should have kept it inside.

Again the airy thunder clapped through the halls. For some odd reason, elementary school hallways seem to be built perfectly for echoes.

"Listen, Lenny. You might want to sit this one out," I said while taking him in the opposite direction, along with the flow of frightened, screaming traffic. "It doesn't look like Drake is in the sharing mood."

"But—"

"It's just that I'm not sure when he'll stop shooting you. Go outside. Watch the door for the bugmen."

"I don't want to go out there alone."

"There's no one there yet. Shit, maybe no one will show."

"I'd...I'll be quiet."

"Can't silence your presence, big guy."

A bullet flew past my ears following my sentence. The impact landed squarely on Lenny's jaw, sending him crashing to the ground.

"Can't say I blame him right now," I continued, helping Lenny sit up. "You're being difficult. Go outside."

Lenny began to continue his plea for innocence, but got distracted by the looseness of his jaw—it just sort of slacked a little lower than normal.

"I know you're not going to do it for me, but he just shot you three times. How many times have you been shot outside?"

He held up his hand to form a zero with his fingers and thumb.

"Now, you haven't been shot out there yet. And well, damn it, Lenny, that's not fair, is it?"

He slowly shook his head. By now, the pain had to have been amplified by the swelling of his fear.

"Get the fuck outside. Now."

Lenny shuffled down the hallway, his dejected, slow body unmoved by the flood of fleeing crowd. Even the crowd didn't see him as a threat.

"The day you chose a different fate...?" I began.

"I spent a long time being the subject of ridicule." Drake went on. "I—"

"Wait. You are not going to attempt the victim-turned-heartless-killer role are you? You're better than a made-for-cable movie."

"Yeah, but Fist of the North Star-caliber," Drake said. He raised the excitement in his voice, hoping the enthusiasm was enough to convince me of whatever he was selling.

"You are without shame,"

"I was vilified for being one of the only Latinos in a black minority-dominated school in a predominately white suburban town. Whitesville, to be exact."

"Now I got to defend all the black people in your fucked up town?"

"There were fourteen Latinos in that school by my count. Every day we got fucked with. Every fucking day. The black...." Drake paused to gauge my reaction.

He was smart enough to know my absence of words did not diminish the signal from my trigger finger tapping my sidearm.

"They would just fuck with us. Call us piss-heads—"

"Isn't that assigned to Arabs?" I asked.

"For the sake of letting the story end, we would all have to walk together. Sit together at lunch and shit. We got close."

"You and the other piss-heads?"

"This story will be told, mijo," Drake pledged.

"Mijo? Mijo? Did you really just call me mijo? Oh, so now you're speaking Spanish? That's the first time you've spoken your native tongue since...what, tenth grade? You got to be shitting me. Come on—cook me a chalupa."

"It never feels natural. Doesn't matter. Irregardless—"

"Okay, see, and now I have to stop you again."

"The fuck, Salt?"

"Saying 'irregardless' is the incest-birthed kin to dropping SAT vocabulary in small talk. I'd rather grate my balls until death or ejaculation before even attempting to go through definitions that you may want to flashcard before attempting 'irregardless' for the masses again. 'Regardless' generally means 'in spite of,' or 'ignoring setbacks, hindrances, or problems.' So basically, everything you just did, but without the fucking 'ir-' to mask or subjugate your general lack of intelligence."

"'Subjugate.' You've been burying that one deep, huh? Go ahead, tell me how you really feel." Drake gestured. He was completely unaffected by my rant, which in hindsight, proved he was that much more intelligent than me.

"Well, what can I say?" I asked with a shrug. "I'm a burier."

"By the way, did you really just quote the dictionary, you fucking first-round spelling bee reject?" Drake could barely control his excitement. He looked like one of the little kids running past us, if one were a drug-fueled sociopath with ill intent, general disregard for reality, and special military training.

"Mira poppi," Drake continued.

"Forcing it," I groaned.

"You know how every clique, no matter what, has a leader? You don't have to wait for conformation of a fucking vote. That shit doesn't happen, but there they are. Sometimes, it's more than one. If you got both sexes in the party, you'd probably get one from both sides. Shit's crazy. I never thought it would break down exactly like some fucking afterschool TV show. Some corny shit, always. But you always get at least one.

"I was in the clique, but I wasn't in the group. I followed, didn't get ordered. One day, Manny starts sitting by me at lunch."

"Was that the Latin king himself?" I asked with as much fake enthusiasm as humanly possible.

"There you go pissing on parades again. Even being a dick right now, you're still not going to knock me off my game, Salt.

"Anyway, Manny was like 'You gotta do something for us, to prove yourself.' Like I had a choice of being Latino?"

"Before today, I never would have known you were Latino."

"He goes on by telling me I got to take out some Asian, Jon Chan or some shit. He was fucking big, though. So, no thing, right? What's a day off of school?"

"You know, I forgot what we were talking about in the first place."

"The next day, coming out for recess, I walked directly up to him, past the sluts, past his crew, past teachers, straight past everyone and right to him. I drilled him right in his chest. I'm not sure what made him choke more—the impact or the shock. Not letting him recover, I rocked his face a couple of times, until I knew he was done, then tackled him to the ground."

"Is it me, or have we been walking forever?" I asked, trying to change the subject.

We had been walking for quite some time. It felt like we saw the last of the fleeing crowd minutes ago, but the hallway appeared to be a thirty-second stroll when we first entered. Even though promptly ignored, it was worth mentioning.

"Before I could get up to stomp him, I was automatically grabbed by the teachers on recess duty—"

"Wait, did you say sluts? What fucking grade was this?"

"Sixth."

In his eyes and lack of expression, I could see he had no clue about my disbelief. Either these girls were lining 'em up in the bathroom since fifth grade, or his exaggeration felt excessively cruel. Almost personal.

"What? Anyway, so the next day, I get back to school. You think I'm gonna be greeted like a hero among my peers. If anything, a couple more hugs from big-titted Maria. But they acted like I rocked one of our own. I went the whole day being ostracized, a frickin pariah."

"Nice job watching the language," I said, nodding to Drake's odd vacation from vulgarity.

"There's kids around," he defended, barely feigning facial concern.

"They are all gone."

"You never know. Anyway, the next day at lunchtime, sitting alone, I feel a tap on my shoulder. Turning to look, I see a fist, then stars. Chan's entire crew was standing behind this kid—Tericho Jones, the popular crew's enforcer. Every popular clique has one to straighten out the non-diplomatic issues, if there is such a thing in grade school."

"But we have sluts? So that's why you hate black people—because of this Tericho?"

"Naw, papi, you're special. I hate you for entirely different reasons. You make me feel all warm inside. Plus, Tericho was from Israel or some shit." Drake added, only to pause at my awkward expression.

Reading my mind, he could see logic was stumbling; the stereotypical Israeli names and descriptions weren't correlating with the names "Tericho" or "Jones."

"Think his mom remarried," Drake went on. "Anyways, I got up and next thing you know, I'm in the adolescent circle of death, surrounded by bloodthirsty twelve-year-olds hell-bent on revenge for Chan. And general apathetic boredom. He proceeded to wipe every inch of that cafeteria's floor with my grill. I held my own, but little matters when your fist is a quarter of the size of his," he said while shadow-boxing against the hallway wall.

I had lost track of how far we had walked. The hallway seemed to stretch for far longer than it seemed appropriate for children to travel to and from class. I didn't even remember the school being that large.

"And then," Drake said, stopping me by waving his hands for effect. "Someone threw a chair."

"A chair?"

"A fucking chair. Came out of nowhere. Up over the circle of bloodthirsty kids and onto the sloppy joe-stained floor. As you can imagine, it ended the fight."

"At any point, and I do mean any, will this get any more fucked up?"

"Yeah, turns out some kid starved for attention threw it cause he thought it would be funny. He was a new kid, so no one laughed. It was fucking funny, though. Everyone just turned around and stared at him. Like, 'who throws a fucking chair'? Not even in a fight. Whatever. The next day, I was allowed back in school I find out that I was setup."

"Tell me there was a phantom shooter!"

"So listen, turns out Enrique Jan Carlos, the alpha dog, didn't like how Marisol thought I was cute. Seeing opportunity, he makes a truce with the cool clique, offering up a sacrificial lamb so to increase their pull."

"So now there's a political plot taking place. Was this before or after spelling and vocabulary block?"

"They were losing a step to the jocks."

"What's incredible is that there's a power struggle going on in an elementary school. Don't have hair on their nuts, but they're swinging dicks. And where was Enrique?"

We finally arrived at the doors that led to the back of the school. Despite my attempt to ignore almost everything the man said, Drake had me intrigued from the chair on. I had to let him finish.

"He was a bitch," Drake went on. "So I was fucking heated. Here I am, championing the betterment of the Latino kind in stuck-up Whitesville Public School, and El Capitan sells me out cause his ugly girlfriend thought I was cute."

"You know something? That is actually fucked up."

"Yeah. So the day after that, before school begins, I walk right up to the Latino section of the playground, and I beat every single one of them. I didn't give a fuck—guy, girl, even Marisol's ugly-ass rat-dog she claimed was a thousand-dollar Chihuahua caught a boot. Because I realized that no matter how hard you try to be loyal and nice, it doesn't fucking matter. There's always gonna be someone who's gonna fuck you. I decided the moment the chair was flipping through the air that that's the last time I'm someone's bitch. From that point on, Enrique Jan Carlos, the Latino section, the rest of the school, and world could lick my grundle."

"It's the way your eye was just twitching that makes me believe you."

"So that's why I may appear to be a bully."

"That, and not things like shooting Lenny in the head?"

"Yeah!"

I just nodded. Futile didn't even begin to describe the attempt to question his logic. Even still, one question just nagged at me until I had to say it aloud.

"Aren't you Portuguese?"

C H . 3 0
THERE'S NO ROOM
FOR ROMANTICS

New Mexico, 2007

Sunday wasn't impressed with my tale of gallant battle between Drake and the redneck messiah, Cleophus. She held it in as best she could until I got to the part about the two dueling with pistols only.

"No. No, no, no." She waved me off. "No."

"What?"

"You did not battle that hero with just sidearms. Bullshit."

"I never said that I did anything. Drake and Cleophus battled."

"And you just stood by?"

"I did, until Drake shot one of the redneck messiah's followers in the head."

"On purpose?"

"Have you met Drake?"

"Why?"

"Cleophus pissed him off. Drake's not big on liars."

"What did he lie about?"

"Well, I was going to tell you, before you got all ancy about it and interrupted me."

"Sorry. What happened next?"

"Fine, I'll tell you. But you know I spoil you, right? I just want you to know that. He dropped his sidearms and began attacking with everything he had. It was a mess."

"So they didn't just battle with sidearms!"

"No. Who does that?"

C H . 3 1
NOT   THE   HERO

Once I was done with my tale of battle against the redneck messiah, which included Drake and the other hero darting all over the sky like God had them on fishing wires in some sick play-in-the-park at that elementary school, and the disappearance of Lenny at the conclusion of said battle, Sunday chose that time to continue to point out how we were really following Lenny that whole time. Understandably, I was skeptical. But don't worry. She let me know the rabbit hole went much, much deeper.

The real problem was that the Battles represented something else. The Employers were looking for beings called Relevants and Recluses. She tried her hardest to explain that these beings, including some heroes, were capable of dimensional travel. And in some cases, some they were capable of creating complete other existences. Civilizations experiencing eons of existence within one being. The Employers knew this, and used it to their advantage.

Having the capability to travel dimensionally as well, the Employers used these beings to cultivate their vast military and reach over all of existence. It was how they were doing what they were with the Battles. Relevants and Recluses eclipsed any known weapon of mass destruction, and could play with the reality of another's created world. Ironically, that was how we—the subjects—really got our nickname, "heroes."

However, some had other effects. Some subconsciously commanded reverence. If not, at least fellowship and remarkable loyalty. Lenny was one of these beings, and according to Sunday, the reason why the Employers were seeking to kill or capture all heroes on Earth.

In hindsight, I should've known the redneck messiah was more than some incredibly charming yet homicidal hillbilly. At the time, I had no real reason to focus on his proclamation that he was worshipped and followed blindly.

"Your boy fucked things up," Sunday went on. "Before him, the Employers were content with just hunting the suspected Relevants and Recluses. But ole Lenny changed the game. Some say he was the first Relevant discovered in the Battles."

"I watched him pee himself when we put him in the trunk."

"Funny part about that. It was that moment that sealed everyone's fate. He was in so much distress during your first battle that while in the trunk, he discovered the power the Employers unleashed during the abduction. He wasn't quiet because he stopped kicking and screaming—it was because he was no longer there."

"Why would I believe any of that?"

"Why?"

"You know, when someone repeats—"

"You know, shut the fuck up, I don't care. The why is simple. The why is because I'm controlling your reality right now. The why is that you know I can appear out of anywhere just to fuck with you, and save your ass—which I remind you, I've done plenty. The fuck do you need a why for? Just listen."

"And now you control my reality?"

"Been doing it since you walked into this bathroom."

"Bullshit."

"No?" Sunday snapped her fingers.

Suddenly, what I mistook for a really long, shitty bass track one of the strippers must have been boring the crowd with turned into the actual song. An unknown male voice responded to Sunday's sidearm—which I thought went off hours ago.

"Just fucking say occupied, next time. Sheesh."

Sunday looked directly at me. She knew I had experienced time slippage before. I had described it to her multiple times.

"What's amazing is that you continue to act like you don't know what it feels like. Every time it happened to you up until meeting me, it was Lenny doing that. He was the one controlling your reality. And before you even fucking ask and make my headache worse, I know because I was also hunting him," Sunday explained.

"You still haven't told me why I should believe you."

Sunday suddenly darted forward and hung one arm tightly around my neck. Before I could even enjoy the smell of pure sex and death wafting from her sweaty body, my attention was brought to her other hand, coming up to my head with an active battlebrace.

She leaned in close, as to kiss me, and whispered, "Don't fucking move."

Her battlebrace blade shot past my head and into something that was apparently behind me. I wanted to ignore it. I wanted to believe it was her fucking with me again, but all bets were off when the dead body of Samytus's right hand, Serrick Cross, hit my leg on the way to the ground.

C H . 3 2
LOST AND FOUND

"Don't worry, it gets worse," Sunday teased as she rested back against the wall and onto my semi-palpable shock. "There was a full day between when you were released from the abductions and when you met Lenny and Drake. Did you notice that when you first met them, the others were walking around like zombies?"

As impossible as it seemed, my mind was ripped away from the body at my feet and to the Common. I saw again the brilliant glare off of Boston's capital dome and a group of people wading around me like zombies.

Never did I once think I was one of them. The scariest part was how easy it was for anyone to just stand in the large park for days at a time. With all the junkies lost in cities, and cities grown to ignore them, the hardest part was believing there weren't more of us.

We were released, and left there the day before I remember standing in place, mentally and physically locked from the abduction itself. Something froze in us, according to Sunday, but not all of us. Some—like Lenny—took to their release immediately.

Though gifted beyond measure, Lenny was no less frightened of any real confrontation. During that first day his abilities were tested, he failed miserably, and was left for dead. That was when

Lenny discovered one of his gifts as a Relevant.

Slipping into what he thought were his death throes, Lenny developed an entire new dimension, then visited it. He settled on a planet very similar to ours, with the only difference being the United States was under a monarchy. A year passed by, then two, then a decade. Before the decade turned, Lenny had amassed a small army of followers. That's when Sunday met him.

"Polis, I think the planet was called. I stumbled on it while testing my own powers. Fell into a love triangle and stayed for a while. Knowing that time on Earth wasn't an issue, I figured, what would it hurt to get laid for a while by two people I'll never have to see again when I'm done with them?"

"And men get shit for wanting to leave in the morning...."

"Morning? Oh honey, most don't make it past me just getting my rocks off."

"Would I get to disappoint you in the morning?"

"No, but back to the love triangle on Polis. Run-of-the-mill drama, as it were. Funny how even in a whole new dimension, love triangles are sticky. What made matters worse was one of them was part of an uprising against the throne, led by an outsider like me named 4lpha."

"I'm not sure what I'm scared of hearing next. Why Serrick is...was here, or that this 4lpha is Lenny."

"Serrick is here because like I told you, Samytus wants to make sure you kill the hero he sent you two here for."

"Why'd you kill him?"

"Mainly to prove a point."

"To me or to Samytus?"

"Would it matter?"

Sunday let her gaze cover me in a snare of seduction and intimidation. Part of me felt like she was exploring my deepest, darkest corners. The parts of my soul that held shameful, almost hateful, thoughts. Thoughts I was scared to even consciously believe I could harbor anywhere within myself.

The other part of me felt like she was looking through me.

Maybe the hundreds, if not thousands, of worlds she had seen by now. I wasn't even sure if she was actually human.

"Your boy, Lenny—or 4lpha, as it were—was quite something. There, he wasn't afraid of conflict. There, he fed off of it."

"So, what happened?"

"He was a rock star. By the time I was done watching him toy with physics and the adulation of his followers, he was poised to take over the North American continent under a banner of pseudo-democracy that, frankly, was really confusing."

"I meant the love triangle."

"Murder-suicide. Really gruesome."

"So Lenny was a superhero in his mind's fake dimension. So what? Why are you telling me this?"

"Do you feel like you are in a fake dimension now? That is the point."

C H . 3 3
STRONG ENOUGH
TO LET YOU LEAD

My mind shot back to the skyscraper in New York. From that point forward, reality began to take a backseat to my desire to survive. More and more, I tested the edges of reality and only grew to seek more boundaries past things I should have been afraid of. It didn't matter if Polite told us there were certain things the activeskin would allow us to do; I had seen enough to know I had no reason to trust anything he, or the Employers, said.

I completely zoned Sunday out and became transfixed on my past battles. I began to see every moment play themselves out— not in rapid, syncopal flashes, but in the same slowed-down pace as when they happened the first time. It was as if I had slipped into an entire dimension of my own. I was lost to Sunday, until she spoke of heroes that rose up under 4lpha appearing in the battles of our reality.

"Your first battle, while Lenny was locked in the trunk, he went back and returned with help. But unlike his time on Polis, where he had developed his powers, here he was still a clumsy novice and scattered his help throughout this dimension. He managed to get two of them close to him, but Lenny's choice in you and Drake proved to be a good one—you two took them out before they could rescue their leader. I believe one even tried to tell you his name."

"Are you going to tell me you were there next, and that is why you know?"

Sunday leaned forward and tapped her finger to my nose in cadence to her response. "That. Is. Very. Good."

"Where? Why? I don't remember seeing you."

"One, I heard your account. You don't remember shit. Two, how good would I be at assassinating people if I made myself known?"

"So now you're an assassin?"

"I'm whatever the fuck I want to be."

"For Samytus?"

The question evoked a little anger from Sunday. She placed her finger inside one of my nostrils. Rather than pulling me to her, it was her to me, but no less painful in execution. Once nose-to-nose, she whispered, "For myself."

"But you were there for him, weren't you? You are here because of him."

Sunday backed off, looking frightened of showing any more emotion. Her eyes darted around as her only show of vulnerability. Then, in the same second, she collected herself.

"We had an understanding. A truce, if you will."

"I think being here, trying to stop his plan, and killing his right hand might put a kink in that."

"He is going too far. He's too powerful for his own good, and ignorant of his devastation. I was, too, until I had to face it head-on."

"I have no clue what you are talking about."

"I didn't find Lenny on Polis, I was sent there. His time creating a dimension, his rise, caused ripples throughout the Realm. Before you ask, that is how the Employers refer to the collective of dimensions and sub-dimensions under theirs. One of those ripples caused a lot of pain in a dimension belonging to the only person I ever believed in. Someone I found during my darkest moment, when this all began. It is because of that, I did what Samytus asked me to do."

"Kill the heroes of the Battles here?"

"Not heroes. That's the thing. Heroes don't exist. One dimension's hero is another's menace. Relevants. Relevants like Lenny that can wield and literally throw dimensions at another being with the same ease as throwing a stone. Those are the ones that matter. Those are the ones Samytus needed me to hunt down to save his own dimensions. Lenny wasn't the first, but he is the first that I hunted who is as powerful as Samytus. I needed to see more of his reach."

"How long had you been at this? I mean, lifetimes?"

"That is what you fail to understand. Time means nothing to the Relevants."

The look on her face brought me to the moment we met.

CH. 34
SHOULD'VE
BEEN CUT OFF

Tennessee, 2006 – I think

Johnston, Tennessee—hub of all things tractor-trailer. An entire city comprised of tractor-trailers hitched on each end to other tractor-trailers, almost creating a fortified circle of trucker bliss. The biggest buildings were the two giant truck stops at the eastern and western most points of the city, with a multitude of twenty-four-hour adult barns and dive bars sprinkled between. Naturally, it felt like a great place to let the world pass us by. In that moment of reflection, Drake and I both agreed that it had been high time we got drunk.

The bar of choice stood out from the rest in that it had fewer tractor-trailer cabs parked out front. The place looked like the strung-out little sister of Dusk Till Dawn's Titty Twister Bar, and even though I made multiple attempts to convince Drake that neither Salma Hayek, nor strippers, nor vampires would be inside, he felt it was the best place to go.

The inside did not disappoint. It was a dive bar that felt decrepit and welcoming at the same time. Nothing was hung with care. Nothing seemed to be in complete working order. The bathrooms were placed way too close to the bar, with a buck hunter videogame placed oddly between them. The bartender wore all his hair in two braids woven out of his long, thick, dirty black beard. When he smiled, he looked like Bam Bam Bigelow during a really bad match. But otherwise, the bar looked empty enough for Drake and me to drink in relative peace.

There was a decent amount of people, but despite its outward appearance, the place was much roomier inside, and so didn't feel cramped at all. Our goal was best sought in relative solitude and discretion. Drake and I knew alcohol could only hide so much. Getting too close to people—"normals" to some heroes, "soft-backs" to Drake—would only prove idiotic and bloody. The normals had long since reverted to a sort of apathy that was often seen in animals surrounded by predators in the wild. They don't want to die, but they aren't going to not live and try to exist.

That didn't mean we needed to force their hand. As I said, our mission was to get sloppy, blackout drunk and hopefully sleep peacefully for the first time in longer than I could remember.

"Barkeep! Four shots of your cheapest whiskey," Drake boorishly ordered as we pulled up to the two unoccupied stools near the shitty TV hanging overhead.

"Who says 'barkeep'?"

"Salt, on most nights, your incessant, cynical poking would bother me on many levels. But not tonight, my friend. For tonight, we get drunk."

Drake slid my two shots over. He took his first two and slammed them down. Not even flinching, he ordered four more. The bartender did not look amused.

Four shots turned into eight, eight into sixteen, sixteen into time becoming obsolete. We sat for ages, drinking, laughing, and cursing our past away. For a brief moment, however long, we were human again. It felt good to remember why alcohol was so necessary to mortality. It was a cheap and unabashed way to not feel scared anymore. Not that we couldn't die anymore, but our deaths would only come with spectacular effort. The normals could die from an errant glass shard in a bar fight that had nothing to do with them. They could simply die on the way home. I missed that feeling.

The crowd had swelled to a respectable gathering for a weekend night, assuming we even knew it was the weekend. It was now a mix of salty townies, the early-shift service industry haunts, and a peculiar scattering of college kids. There was a university or some crap about ten miles out. Thankfully, the alcohol placed blinders on the visual salad of rebel flag attire and popped pastel colors.

Behind Drake stood the image of the prototypical cornhusker—big, strong, corn-fed boy with a blond flattop to square off his rotund, yet similarly square face, as if his bulbous visage was barely held in by an invisible frame. He stood like Captain America and expected to get noticed. I was already a fan, but Drake was harder to please. Inexplicably, the man began to tap Drake on the left shoulder.

"Hey, buddy."

Drake ignored him.

"Hey. Buddy," the man continued with more tapping

Drake continued to ignore him.

"Hey," a new voice said into my right ear.

Reformed punk rocker disguised in a white cardigan, pink polo, and green skirt. She must have eased in next to me. She owned the new look as if the former was the real disguise, but the rose vine tattoos and facial piercings showed her true favor. Her brown skin smelled of sex and death, but her eyes burned of compassion.

I was in love before she even opened her mouth. I'd ruined every woman that I'd been in love with. Lucky for her, I am horrible with women.

"I'm horrible with women," I said. It was more like my mind puked and my words were the result.

"That's what you lead with?" she asked. Her right eyebrow arched in amazement. "Gonna buy me a drink, cool boy?"

"I haven't bought shit all night, but sure. What's your poison?"

"What's yours?"

"Well...." I paused to stare at the last drop left in my glass. "Pretty sure this was cheap whiskey.

"Then whiskey it is," she responded.

And there it started. She slammed them back harder than Drake and laughed off the whiskey kickback with a deep bellow that held no fear. And like Drake, shots multiplied fast and our conversation roared on.

"Does this mean we talk all night and you fall in love with me afterwards, cause I gotta tell you, I'm a little bit of a heartbreaker. I'll hatefuck you."

"Eww, promises. Let's start with a name," she said with a smile.

"Salt."

"Salt?"

"Salt."

"Your name is Salt?" she asked once more.

"What? Not meeting your approval? What's yours?"

"Sunday."

"And you're giving me shit?"

"What? There's nothing wrong with the name Sunday."

"Not saying there is. Just saying it's no more common than being called Salt, especially if it's not the first name. So, weirdo girl with weird name, what's your story?"

"I'm just a churchgoing Christian waiting for a fucking shot."

It was hard to ignore her absolutely natural church girl beauty. She had it. Almost too much, which made her persona, her tattoos, and piercings even more decadent. I had dreamt about her; just never knew it.

"Fair enough. Bartender," I said, trying to flag him down.

"I think your friend is in some shit," Sunday said, motioning over to Drake.

I had completely ignored him—and the rest of the bar, for that matter. It was as if nothing at all existed, or at least didn't necessarily exist in the same plane we did once she locked eyes with me. The world could have ended at that moment, and I would have been okay with it.

But behind me, the square-faced man continued with more and more violent animation. "What the fuck, man? I just want to ease in and be next to my friends!"

"Fuck Drake. So what's with the reform?" I asked Sunday, ignoring Drake's potential blood bath in the process.

"Who said it's reform?"

"The cardigan and schoolgirl skirt do."

"No, that's what my mood is telling you," she corrected.

"Then what's my mood telling you?" I asked.

"In order?"

"Sure?"

"You have a heavy soul, you are concerned about your friend's lust for death, you want to fuck me, and you are really drunk," she answered robotically.

"To be fair, I had a head-start."

"So you say," she toyed. "More shots before your friend gets killed and raped by that maniac cornhusker?

C H . 3 5
BETTER YET, PRAY FOR VAMPIRES

At this point, he was spitting onto the side of Drake's face. Remarkably, Drake continued to stare forward. But his smile was at the point where everyone dies.

"Bartender, some shots, please!" I pleaded with authority.

"Fuck you! Fuck! You!" the man hollered into Drake's ear.

"Some fucking shots, please!" I yelled.

At that point, I felt something snap. It was in the air. I could hear it. I couldn't see it, and it wasn't a flash. I just felt like everything was different.

"You'll remember me when the westward wind moves upon the fields of holly!"

"The fuck...?" Drake asked.

"Where I'll be kicking your ass!" the man yelled. His lungs gurgled with blood and mouth foamed with spit.

"You gotta be shitting me," I said.

The man reached for Drake's left battlebrace. The bartender whipped out a battleshotgun from behind the bar and cocked it. Sunday smiled, and then everything went white.

When we came to, the entire bar was covered in blood. Everything either had blood or guts or some other piece of a person dripping from it. The entire room felt and sounded like a sweat bath if it ran on blood and guts. Hellraiser himself would need a moment to get his composure from what we were standing in. Checking the bodies, as I verbally spewed, was really a matter of academics.

"Check the bodies," I demanded.

"Let's get the fuck out of here!" Drake shouted back. Even he looked disturbed.

"Check the bodies!"

"Why? Do you want to dance with whatever did this?"

"I give less than two rat shits about that. We're still here. Check the bodies."

"Why? What the fuck do you care? They're dead heroes and softbacks—nothing new."

"Did you just walk in and jump into the fight? Did you not hear what that raving lunatic said before all this happened? Is it even fucking occurring to you that we were in a bar with probably multiple heroes here waiting for us? We are just wondering around the fucking country, and there are people organized enough to set an ambush for us! Check the fucking bodies."

I didn't even want to think of why the man thought to reach for Drake's battlebraces. We hadn't a clue what happened there, just that everyone was dead, and I had a feeling it was because of a smile.

"And what is it you hope to find? Where are the answers going to be applied to gain you any insight?" Drake demanded.

"Heroes die different than normals, right?"

"I'm not going through the checklist with you. You're looking for that girl," Drake snapped, smiling proudly at his minor discovery of intent.

"Her, too. She plays a part in this, too."

"How you figure?"

"Because I think she fucking knew this was coming."

"I did. Sorry, I had to step out for some reds," Sunday said while tapping the bottom of her cigarette box.

"That's not setting a good example for the kids. Mind if I get one?" Drake gleefully stepped toward her. He reached out in eager anticipation of his cancer stick.

"Leave it alone, Salt," Drake said in anticipation of my disdain toward cigarette smoking. Cigarette clinging to his lips, he muttered, "The government made it possible from thin air. Everything gives us cancer."

He leaned forward to let Sunday light it with both the lighter and the same intoxicating grin that fucked me before.

"You two really don't have a clue about what's going on, do you?" she asked.

"What happened here? Did you arm everyone and make them kill each other in a sick orgy of death for your amusement?"

"What?" Sunday snapped.

"Did you arm the softbacks, darling?" Drake asked.

"Not my thing, but you can thank me for being alive," she said with a smile.

"What happened?" I asked.

"Bartender put two into Drake's chest, then one in the cornhusker's head," she answered. "Then shit got ugly."

"That's where that itch came from," Drake said to himself, rubbing at the chest.

"Yeah. Almost didn't make it. Loverboy over here actually pulled his gun on me, but I was already off battling, so he cleared out all the people behind me. The softbacks were armed, but only five were heroes, so not so bad."

Drake clapped. "Atta boy."

"How long did the battle last?" I asked.

"To me, or to them?"

"Meaning?"

"Meaning you are not focusing on the right questions."

"Here's a question. Why aren't we dead? Better still, why didn't you attack us?" I asked.

C H . 3 6
FORGET ABOUT
GOOD NEWS

New Mexico, 2007

"Why did you save us?" I asked, waiting until I locked eyes with her.

Her eyes were still restless. Being mistaken as property of another appeared to be the only thing that got to her. If only I knew enough about her to protect myself.

It was then that I realized I had just been standing there, not saying a word. I was locked in the memory of meeting her, and hung on a question I had hoped to ask her once Drake and I came to. But the more I looked at her, the more I remembered she was nowhere to be found.

That was the last time I saw her before she decided to interrupt a tense misunderstanding between myself and an Alt gunship. The misunderstanding was that the gunship was trying to kill me, and I did not want to die. It was just another time Sunday saved us—noble in the moment, but horrifying in the abstract.

It was an impossible hurdle to clear—the fact that someone who had shown up out of nowhere twice to save two people her associate needed in the future. If that associate had the clairvoyance to send Sunday after us back when this all started, then he must have seen Sunday's insurrection, yet did nothing to stop it.

No matter how this conversation ended, if I actually decided to brush my teeth with stripper bathroom toothbrush, or the hero we were sent here to kill ended up alive after today, I was fucked. Was Sunday saving us only for us to meet Samytus, or to prevent what he wanted us to do? Regardless of the intent, she was never around to answer why—until now.

"The day I met you, Drake and I woke up in that bar as the only ones alive. What happened?"

"What do you think happened?"

"I feel like the bartender attacked Drake and the kid, then everything went white."

"Close, but it's funny you were thinking about that day. That was the day I knew Lenny was still alive, and chose to continue following you two, instead of just finally killing you and crossing more names off my list."

"Thanks?"

"Thank Lenny."

"I'm still not seeing it—this Lenny thing. And why'd you need us if you really wanted Lenny? He wasn't with us when you saved us in Chicago."

"It wasn't 'us,' it was you. And I did it because I wasn't ready to see you die just yet."

"Grown sweet on me, huh? I know. It's the charm. You know, my mo—"

"Stop. Please. Before you let your ego get any bigger, it was because I still couldn't find Lenny."

"I mean, I get that, but—"

"Do you? Because once Lenny disappeared after your little elementary school showdown, no one could find him."

"Then what about that night told you otherwise, sparing our lives as a merciful result?"

"Don't be so dramatic."

"We are talking about you killing me as a possible outcome of the first time we met."

"Death isn't everything."

"No, cause you don't want to die."

"Don't assume."

"Then why fight? Why not just lay down and die? Let life seep out of you?"

"Because I fucking despise not having that choice. I knew Lenny was around because of the bartender. He was a hero in Lenny's uprising on Polis. I didn't recognize him until I saw his battleshotgun. A customized BS-Seiger Nine from one of Lenny's greatest hero's sub-dimension. That gun had a lot of blood attached to it."

"So Lenny is just creating heroes all over the place?"

"You need to stop looking at this whole thing as simple cause and effect, as what Lenny is. What he represents is something only beings like what most call "God" would possess. Relevants don't just create dimensions and that's it. When a Relevant creates a dimension, whether on purpose or not, life is created along with it. Timelines of civilizations begin and exist all within the Relevant's creation. It is real, and it can be exploited by higher forces, just like here."

"Are you telling me Lenny became the Employer to his own dimension? Are you telling me that is what is happening here?"

"I'm telling you I knew the bartender, not because I remembered him distinctly from the uprising, but from traveling through one of the dimensions created by a powerful hero in Lenny's uprising. A hero cultivated by Lenny."

"Didn't you kill the bartender?"

"I didn't say I liked him, or was happy to see him. Shit got real because he finally noticed some of the heroes that followed you to the bar were part of Samytus's group—a rival group, of course, to Lenny."

"But not you?"

"What about me makes you think I'd get noticed by that specimen, with the balding head and Hulk Hogan blond beard woven into two long braids? I said I noticed him."

"Ha! His beard was black."

"You can't handle your liqueur because you don't remember shit. It was blond."

"Wait, there were more than just you following Drake and me?"

"Let's just say by that point, Samytus and I had already grown to differ on a few nonstarters."

"Like?"

"Like mind your own fucking business, how bout that?"

"This whole thing is about me and Drake!"

"Drake, really, but yeah—me following the two of you for Lenny is about the two of you. Don't you worry your pretty dumb head about Samytus and me."

"Ahh, mommy doesn't want to tell me why you and daddy might get a divorce. I won't blame myself, I promise."

"You should. It doesn't matter, because the point is Lenny had made himself visible, which meant I still needed you."

"Why was Lenny so important to you?"

"The problem with being a Relevant isn't the godlike power over dimensions; it is the weight of it all. As I said, life is created when a Relevant creates a dimension. Recluses are powerful, sure, but can only visit other dimensions. Most do what we call 'slipping' because they don't even know when it happens, or what they potentially can do when they come back."

"The man in the reggae cave?"

"Yes, but he was on the more powerful side of the spectrum. He knew exactly what he was doing. But more to the point, when he was killed, it was just he that died. When a Relevant dies, it takes all the life that it creates with it."

"So you were hunting Lenny to kill all the life he created?"

The horror of that thought was hard to shake. Were we killing souls by the billions one hero at a time?

"At first, yes. There are wars being fought in lower dimensions that have real consequences in ours. The heroes that came here from Lenny's dimension were potential Relavants containing dimensions that caused great strife in Samytus's. Killing them could have ended a lot of suffering."

Sunday looked away, shaking her head. This was the only moment of vulnerability she had ever fully shown me. The other times were mere flirtations. The weight of not only her actions, but the actions of all of us involved, crushed her.

"But all that changed?" I asked her.

"It was easy to lose track of time when travelling through those lower dimensions belonging to Relevants. I spent lifetimes there. I've seen and done so much. Loved and hated enough to fill a hundred lifetimes. But the first one was spent with Samytus.

"Like Lenny, my first slip was in a moment of distress during my first battle. I just dropped to my knees in the middle of the street while others battled around me. All I could do was scream and cover my head with my hands. I wanted to scream myself into death. I hoped my pain from screaming so hard would distract me from finally being killed.

"When I stopped screaming, I saw Samytus. From there, he showed me a reality only gods were meant to know. He showed me how to find the power within myself to make the Employers secondary to my focus on life, instead of being trapped by their design. He showed me some of those lifetimes I just mentioned, and he did it all span of a day. That's when we met Verona and everything changed."

"Verona? The little hell-spawn I talked about?" I asked. Sunday had no problem speaking of killing countless of people, but her forced show of respect for that little girl was glaring.

She nodded. "Even now, I feel it is impossible to know for sure if she was released from the abductions like the rest of us, or a product of our exploits in the lower dimensions. Wherever she came from, she was one of the most powerful any of us had come across.

"We met her while exploring one of Samytus's failing dimensions. It was one of his first, made during a time when he really didn't know what his actions would do to everything under his control. The civilizations within it had grown quite intelligent, but their animus and hate was causing collapses in the neighboring dimensions. Not necessarily a painful loss to Samytus—even by the second day, his reach was approaching a dozen dimensions. But his pride, that was different.

"When we started our investigation into the root of the failing dimensions, several of the dimensions' planets identified an 'alien' race of similar-looking beings intervening in their war—unabashedly siding with the most vulnerable in the war and destroying Samytus's dimensions causing massive collaspes. We followed that alien race back to their home dimension, only to discover it belonged to a hero here on Earth."

"Verona," I interjected.

I was amazed I could say anything at all with my brain doing it's best to conceptualize so much existence within something I had killed. I had a whole new reason to want revenge for my new fate. We are monsters. I am a monster.

"Not even close," Sunday replied. "I wish this all were that neat. No, it led us to a hero that belonged to Verona. It took some time to trace it all back to that little girl, but even then, we were left with questions."

"So, beings from a being within Verona were powerful enough to create a dimension powerful enough to reach a dimension of Samytus's? How was this even possible?"

"It was only inevitable for beings of Relevant dimensions to find each other. It is all connected. Whether by space travel or dimensional, if it exists, it can be travelled to. The strident child had so much control, I could see she unnerved Samytus. But instead of killing her right away, he offered protection. Verona was resistant at first, considering she had done well on her own since getting released. She told us to fuck off the first time. But she quickly understood Samytus's reach when he sent me to one of her dimensions to destroy it while he asked her to reconsider."

"If they were allies, then why did he let us kill her?"

"That, my little dumbfuck, is the reason for our divorce."

C H . 3 7
READY FOR THE FLOOR

The dimension reflects the Relevant. That is how Sunday explained the underlining aura found in each Relevant's dimensions. She saw how each one, including the sub-dimensions, found infinite ways to express themselves in blind reverence for their creator.

Verona's dimensions were the most valiant. All her civilizations rose up to be grand and just protectors of the weaker species they would encounter as they began to explore the Realm.

Polis, an otherwise insignificant little planet thought to belong to a lost dimension, changed everything. Finding out nothing was 'lost' about the dimension, and that it belonged to a Relevant powerful enough to hide ownership of it while existing in it, was only the start of the tidal wave that shifted the current of Sunday's trust and focus.

"Lifetimes. I spent lifetimes in Verona's dimensions," Sunday went on. "They were absolutely fascinating. That little girl must've had a fantastic imagination. Such a shame. There was one species in her dimensions that had two races, and the only difference between the two was that one was born to be the silent protector of the other. The Uusa, I think. Magnificent species, beautiful people."

She wandered off as she thought back to her time within

Verona's dimensions. The light in her eyes danced with each treasured experience that came to mind as she continued to recollect.

"If you were following us by the time we battled her, why didn't you stop us?" I asked.

"Right before I returned from my last trip into her dimensions, I led one of her species into a war to protect a planet that was about to be taken over by species from an Earth Relevant's dimension. A Relevant that had successfully hunted down several heroes of Samytus's. Heroes that were responsible for a quarter of Samytus's might.

"The species I led successfully defended the planet. But instead of leaving with them, something told me to defy Samytus's request to return. I faked my own death to begin a new life there on the planet. Things were god-awful boring until my third lifetime. That is when Lenny showed up. I didn't know who he was until he began the uprising, using powers invisible to the beings on that planet, but glaring to a Relevant or Recluse—and to the Employers.

"After his successful uprising, he guided that planet back to prosperity, and eventually intergalactic travel. His success gained the attention of the Employers. Polis, now thousands of years into their future, had countless species from multiple dimensions willing to stand with them and fight, but only one of his allies had the might and courage to save them."

"Verona's," I answered.

"I hate myself for listening to Samytus that day. The three of you were dead. You were never going to make it to the street that little girl found herself on that day, but he came to me right after I returned to kill you three. Samytus was convinced letting you battle her would result in more good than bad. He forced me to watch his version of the future where Verona lives, but the eventual war lost defending Polis would result in unparalleled loss of life compared to the trillions lost with only Verona's death."

Sunday looked down and swallowed hard before continuing. "I watched you fools luckily take out a warrior that may have been the savior for us all. I'm letting you live to make that up."

It was in that moment I truly felt like I knew what she was thinking, where she was going with this visit. Samytus wasn't out to destroy the Employers in his own way, as we all were. He had joined them.

"That bastard knew I had seen just enough to know his future was beyond possible," Sunday said. "But in reality—in ours, at least—Verona was more of a threat to the Employers than any of us. Everything has gone to shit since you killed her. Forget about her dimensions, her reach was already so great that her removal allowed the Employers to hunt down every species posing any threat to them. Most went through the same hell we are going through, but with fewer mistakes like us.

"My allegiance will never be with the Employers. My sole purpose as I breathe is to kill every last of one them," Sunday declared. "Samytus saw what the fall of Verona would wreak. That was the last time I would be his pawn as he fools himself into partnership with the Employers, when really he is their proxy. Fuck that, and fuck him. What was also clear was that Samytus wanted Lenny to fall, which meant I needed to know more about him."

A cold chill developed deep within my spine, then travelled throughout my body so completely it replaced my central nervous system. I was on the wrong side of a being so powerful he saw lifetimes ahead to make sure his most trusted and powerful ally will be exactly where he needs her to be thousands of years into the future. He could see the one thing to convince her to continue helping him—if only for one more favor.

On one hand, all of this was impossible. On the other hand, thinking of the day Lenny came back into our lives was just that.

C H . 3 8
THE FIRST DINOSAUR TO FALL (NOT WARM)

Minnesota, 2006

We were standing in the middle of Minneapolis, in January's ass. Mr. Polite mentioned the activeskin would serve some heating purpose, but against two below, it seemed nothing more than an extra thermal undershirt—otherwise known as "fucking nothing."

"It's fucking cold," Drake snapped.

We stood like two dorks playing arctic military dress-up, thanks to a successful raid on Dick's Sporting Goods—complete with the shine-action ski goggles and headbands. Drake chose the dark urban military fatigue, double goose down coat with the wooly hood. With the hood up, he looked like Brutus from the Popeye cartoon coming from a pep rally. He was even chewing his gum so obnoxiously that every loud smack was like a light flashing on and off.

Why were we there? For the most part, no reason. But the rumors of a hero bringing an atomic winter to a city—and just that city—pulled at my curiosity to such insane levels that it almost overtook the overarching question of my new existence—how do I get my revenge against the Employers.

At this point, I had said goodbye to the "why" of what was happening to me—being a hero, that is—or the others that were abducted. Time with Drake had changed that.

It's impossible to summarize the ravings of a drug–fueled sociopath, but it pretty much went something like: "Who gives a shit? The most probable outcome is that it will be still under-whelming to the loss we suffer to become what they wanted us to be. The 'why' is whatever the fuck you want it to be.".

Which brings us here. If the rumors were even half-true, then that meant there was a hero here that either knew more on how to get to the Employers, or that the Employers were allowing to be there.

"Why are we here, Salt?"

"You know why?"

"RocketjoyL0ve? Fuck that guy. He's a myth."

"At this point, we are all myths to any normal that survives our battles."

"Not enough. I'm getting tired of hunting down every poor fuck like us you think has gone supervillain."

He only partially had a point. Our travels had been guided somewhat by different rumors of heroes with incredible power since meeting Sunday. None of them had any power close to hers. Most of the rumors we tracked were more like the hero who chose to reside in his own room. People said they were strong, but oddly focused. One had super strength, but feared fighting alone. Another could see the future seconds ahead, but made really bad decisions.

RocketjoyL0ve was different. No rumor could claim the "how," but multiple placed him as the reason Minneapolis has been evacuated completely, and for its steady fall of ash-like snow. The rumor that intrigued me more than the others was the tale of him shooting down a nuclear strike on the city.

"Doesn't concern you at all that this hero had cleared out an entire city and has just stayed here unnoticed by Alt, huh?"

"How do you know he has been ignored? Maybe he's that

fucking good," Drake countered.

"We've been in the city for about an hour now. Not one sign of a battle, especially one with the Employers."

The eerie silence and dead gray sky was imposable to ignore. Nothing moved.

"Every day looks like this." A broken voice from out of nowhere broke into our conversation.

And there he was, the infamous RocketjoyL0ve. I knew it immediately from seeing each of his arms fused to devastational cubes. Past that, he was not what I was expecting. He was a broken man, doubled over both to nurse his weary arms from carrying the extended rocket launchers all the time—as all rumors pointed out—and from what looked like a shattered soul.

"The fucking gardener," Drake said. He seemed slightly disappointed, as if he, too, expected something…bigger.

"I beg your pardon?" the man hushed.

"Well, not for nothing, but have you looked at yourself? You are the spitting image of the stereotypical Latino gardener," I said, pointing to his green pants, puffy yellow vest, Walmart flannel jacket pulled over a smaller flannel shirt, and his oddly immaculate mesh Phoenix Suns hat.

"It is negative ten," the man defended. His speech did, in fact, have a thick Latino accent.

"So?" Drake asked.

"So, what?" the man replied.

"So, what are you?"

"Is that even relevant?"

"I'm not the one that got all offended at being called a gardener while looking like a fucking gardener."

"I have a relevant question," I said. "Why are you here?"

"This is my hell."

"Okay, now we kill him," Drake exclaimed as he raised his battlerifle.

"You poor fuck," RocketjoyL0ve said. "You think you can? Go ahead, but does it bother you that I'm the only one you've seen for hours?"

"So you've been following us?" I said while trying to lower Drake's weapon.

"Fuck you, Salt. Don't touch my rifle."

"He can keep it raised. Fire it, too. I've survived worse."

"Okay, that's the second cryptic thing you said," I said.

"Do you want to talk or battle?" RocketjoyL0ve asked.

"Battle," Drake answered.

"Talk before battle?" I offered. "How bout that? Drake can finish his blunt, and you can tell me why you welcomed us to your hell."

"I don't need to wait, Salt—I just chomp down on it harder," Drake shrugged off. His comment was just met with an annoyed stare from both RocketjoyL0ve and me.

"Right. Well, I'm gonna guess and say you are Rocket-joyL0ve." I signaled that my navguide no longer had a read.

"Yes," he answered.

"Are you responsible for all this?"

"Yes."

"Why? How?"

"Fuck you. I don't answer to you two." He spat at us.

"You are right. But we are here, and no one is dead yet, so why not the company for a minute or two?"

"Why do you care?"

"We don't," Drake barked.

"What he means is your life's story. What I mean is, why aren't you being hunted down by the Employers like the rest of us and allowed to stay here?"

It seemed like the idea of actually carrying on a conversation with another person was beginning to entice him. He gave a few more seconds, and then sat down cross-legged, resting his rocket arms awkwardly across them.

"They don't come anymore," he whispered with more defeat than volume in his voice.

C H . 3 9
PARDON MY SAVIOR

Miraculously, Rocketjoyl0ve had lost the interest of the Employers—or so he said. He remembered a time when they came, when they hunted him, but he couldn't remember the last time. What he did remember was far worse.

"I killed my wife and my rival/partner the day of the abduction," he began. "I found them, in my lab. Looking back at it, I think it was their favorite spot. Why not? I was in my office after 7:00 p.m., never home. That was just where I slept and forgot about her. In the end, all this time away, I forgive her. I pushed her to him.

"When I found them, I think they tried to explain. I didn't hear anything really, just watched their lips move as I went deaf with indifference. I don't remember much after that, other than looking down and seeing my mangled hands carving the innards of lifeless bodies. It wasn't until I broke a finger on the floor, having reached through their bodies, that I realized what I had done. I got up, incinerated everything, including my clothes, raided the lost and found bin in my office, and set the sequence for the emergency response shuttle housed underneath the university."

"Alright, I got to stop you there," Drake waved off. "I was bored as shit and wasn't paying attention, but did you just say, 'shuttle'?"

"Yes. This university and several others were part of a secret governmental doomsday program, which included multiple shuttles that could orbit the earth for a decade. I was the lead scientist on the quantum reactor that propelled the shuttle. I was going to take the shuttle."

"You are heartless," I said in slight disbelief.

"Truth be told, I thought the whole plan was beyond idiotic. If there were an event that happened on a doomsday level to this planet, we would need far longer than a decade to ride it out. I did it for the engine my team created. I was going to be the next science world rock star."

"But of course, I never made it. The abductions made sure of that. But at nightfall of the first day of our release, I got myself to the highest rooftop I could find and waited for the shuttle to take off. Knowing the devastation an explosion from the quantum reactor would cause, and hoping to end it all, I shot it down."

"Fuck off," Drake jumped in.

"Excuse me?"

"Look. You had me at going Mr. Jackal on your wife and her lover. Hell, I was down for you being an actual rocket scientist and not the gardener you currently look like. But shooting down a shuttle? That's like—"

"Hitting a missile with a bullet? Yeah it is. Like I said, I was going to be a fucking scientist rock star."

"Hence the atomic winter?" I asked.

"Sadly beautiful, isn't it. Maybe the world wouldn't be so bad without us."

"Everything dies in this shit, you lunatic," Drake corrected.

"I meant no difference."

"Except for you?" I asked.

"This is my hell," he answered. "I went to sleep after watching that spectacular explosion in the heavens. When I awoke to this winter wonderland, every living thing was gone. Every day has looked exactly the same."

He pointed down the street. "Day forty three. Battle with the

Alt left that entire block decimated."

Not only was there nothing destroyed, it hit me that there should've been a lot more snow on ground.

"Just last week, I battled some hero that left the whole city razed. But it's not just that. I died during that battle."

"One more time?"

"Died. Dead. Gone. The hero brought in a whirlwind of pain behind her, including the Alt. The battle lasted for hours, but in the end, she got me after I thought I got the last Alt gunship keeping us pinned down. I remember the pain. I remember the fight against keeping my eyes closed. I remember darkness colder than I thought I could bear. And then I awoke here. That's when I knew I was cursed with eternity.

"Since then, I've been shot, stabbed, maimed, mangled, rolled, and crushed. I've snuck aboard Alt transports, jumped out once we were damn near in space, only to awake right where I always do—the rooftop I slept the night of the shuttle."

"Can you leave?"

"No. Nothing changes for me."

The weight of his words collapsed his shoulders and made him appear as if he had given up. "Not so much for you, though. Everyone else always dies."

Showing uncanny grace, RocketjoyL0ve used his rocket arms to propel himself up into the air. He flew towards a building's side, then continued to use his rockets against different buildings to disappear over the city's skyline.

"Conversation over?" Drake mused,

His question was met by a shower of rockets from the skies, sending us running for cover in opposite directions.

Everywhere I ran, I could either hear his laugh, or had a rocket nip at my heels. He was everywhere.

Drake and I came to an intersection several blocks away just in time to see RocketjoyL0ve hover over us. It was unreal how many rockets he had. He propelled himself upward, then aimed both arms at us.

Truth be told, I hadn't a clue what I was going to do next. More to the point, it was the first time I had witnessed Drake's level of not giving a fuck reach the point of not even wanting to get out of the way of almost certain death. Then again, knowing Drake, he could've easily have questioned if that was the actual intent of something that toyed with us for several blocks now.

In fact, RocketjoyL0ve could have killed us at any time, but we were all deprived of that fate when a transport dropped out of nowhere, landing with a thud that teased of the ship comically falling apart, and with RocketjoyL0ve underneath it.

"That just happened..." I whispered, more to myself from sheer shock.

"Okay, Salt. Now I'm beginning to see your point on this whole 'there's something more to this' thing," Drake said.

"Gotta be honest with you—not at any point in my daily rants of existential assignation of our souls at the hands of malevolent spacemen did I see a battle ending with a ship suddenly landing on a hero's head."

The transport's bay doors opened. An approaching image began to materialize through some dramatic mist. Not very tall. Not at all in shape. With every step, it got worse and worse, until the figure standing in front of us looked a lot like Lenny.

C H . 4 0
As a Fiend Would

New Mexico, 2007

Now was my time to get caught up in raw emotion. I lost myself in remembering someone I simply didn't appreciate when he was around, dimension-creating power be damned. In the oddest, and most painful way, it hurt more to think of the short but wild times he, Drake, and I had in the beginning of the Battles than it did my own family.

I couldn't miss my family and friends of my past life more, but with so much to mourn at once, that pain got trapped and hardened around my soul, turning it into something unforgiving and alien to my own consciousness. In many ways, the part that mourned them died with them, but what was left could only accept so much, and let go of even less.

"You thought he was dead, didn't you?" Sunday asked, reading right through my attempt to look unaffected.

"Wouldn't you, if you didn't know what you know?"

"Probably."

"We treated him like shit."

"You did."

"And he just took it."

"Yeah."

"Why?"

A little thrown off in my sudden jump in emotion, Sunday gave me a second before answering. "Never figured that out."

The Boston Common came back to me with such intensity everything else was gone, even Sunday. All I could see was what I saw before—the subjects zombified by shock, anger, and grief, getting lost in the sea of people that filled the Common each day. Then I saw the conversation Drake and Lenny were having before they approached me. I still couldn't hear anything, and I suck at reading lips, but everything they said to each other felt known to me, as if I directed them to talk. But that was a curse, because even with such clarity, I still didn't know what they actually said.

"The conversation in the Common?"

"What?"

"When I met Lenny and Drake, they were talking to each other about something."

"And?"

"I haven't a fucking clue."

"And how is that helpful?"

"You said I was basically frozen in shock for a day, but Drake and Lenny already knew each other. Do you think Lenny needed us?

"No. And up until Lenny dying, I was convinced Drake was from him."

"What the fuck?"

"Think about it. You said it yourself—they knew each other before approaching you."

"They also could've just met."

"Sure could, but would that make more or less sense in your reality these days? Keep in mind, your soulmate, Drake, is out there thinking it has only been about long enough for you to be taking a shit."

"With Lenny dead, what do you think now?" I asked.

"There's nothing to think. Drake is still here."

"Is that why he came back? He needed us then?"

I was beginning to look more and more to Sunday for answers. Nothing and everything she said made sense to me. Her ability to stand in the hurricane of events we found ourselves in and be able to identify order became the only thing my soul could latch onto. Even if she was lying, even if she had no fucking clue what she was talking about and making most of this up, it was all I had. I was beginning to notice that, as a fiend would their choice dependence.

"You tell me, cowboy. What did he say?"

"'I thought you were dead.'"

C H . 4 1
SEEMINGLY NOTHING

Minnesota, 2006

"Thought you guys were dead," Lenny announced as he bounded down the ship's boarding strip.

He looked good—almost too good for someone we assumed to have been dead. He looked like he was much better off without us.

"I'm officially quitting drugs," Drake mumbled.

"That will hold. That can't be you, Lenny," I said as I continued to stare at him after he released us from his bear hug. I was waiting for him to dissipate, as mirages do.

"We have much to discuss," Lenny forced through a giant smile.

Drake and I looked at each other, then the transport. We generally had nothing to lose, and I couldn't speak for Drake, but I was dying to see what one of those things looked like from the inside. With a shrug and a wince, we climbed aboard.

It was outstanding in its simplicity. From the outside, most of the standard transports we saw looked like the inside of a giant pantyhose egg; hollow and plain. I almost shat myself when I saw it was the same from the inside.

Open and stark-white, like the cell from my dream during

the abduction, there was nothing to greet us but an almost unobstructed view of the outside from the cockpit.

"Sit. Relax." Lenny motioned as he moseyed up to the front of the cockpit. He sat down in a chair that appeared once he began to bend his knees. "Trust me, the view is treating you well right now, but she is an unforgiveable bitch the first few times we get cookin'."

Joining him, we sat down into seemingly nothing as chairs appeared like they did for Lenny. The craft lifted off with the same thrust as a leaf riding the wind off the ground. In seconds, the city was lost underneath the blanket of white atomic clouds.

Lenny made a few key sequences with his hands on panels that only appeared when his hand reached the area, then stood up to face us.

"You guys are hard to find. I was beginning to give up hope," Lenny started.

"So, Lenny. What's going on? I asked, dumbfounded.

"Let's wait until we get to our destination. I'll be able to ensure we will be alone there. No one there but us."

"I feel like that shouldn't be our first concern while we are flying around in an alien spacecraft," I returned.

"I've missed you guys!" Lenny said as he jollily strolled past us to look out the side of the craft. "Man, this planet has the best horizons."

"Been busy, chubby?" Drake poked.

"I've even missed that. You don't know how far some of those tough life lessons you taught carried me in the life I've had since we last saw each other."

"Life? It's been like four fucking months."

"Something like that," Lenny dismissed.

"Lenny. Where have you been?" I asked.

"In some shit, man."

"What do you mean?"

"It'd be better if I showed you."

His words directed us to an epic flock of the most opaque

clouds I had ever seen. The white hue was so overwhelming it created illusions of shadows and shades of blue. It was then that I noticed we were flying towards them.

A few seconds later, a fortress of incredible towers and spires appeared. Colossal rings surrounded and rotated around the entire fortress.

Drake didn't see the splendor in it all, and immediately brought his battleshotgun up to Lenny's head. Lenny let out an uneasy chuckle that evaporated all the bravado he had been mustering since dropping the transport on RocketJ0ylove.

"Drake?" I asked, hoping to find out what he was thinking before he potentially killed our only other friend in the world.

"Take another look at that fortress, Salt. Something look or feel familiar? How about why this craft is stylistically similar to that floating monster gyroscope? It's a fucking setup!" Drake barked.

I was willing to ignore Drake's conspiracy and talk him down, but beyond the coincidence of Lenny's craft looking like it was made by the same beings that created this cloud fortress, the fact that Lenny knew where this place was, and the eerie, unshakeable feeling that I had been there before, it was Lenny's sheepish grin and laugh that turned me toward believing Drake. I showed my support by holding a battlebrace blade up to Lenny's throat.

"It's not what you think," Lenny tried to say calmly.

"Yeah? What do we think, chubby?" Drake demanded.

"That I'm taking you to the Employers."

Drake responded by letting a round off towards the craft's roof. Instead of piercing the hull, or even ricocheting, the round simply absorbed into the material of the craft. It didn't stop both Lenny and I from taking a break to stare at Drake as if he had lost his mind.

"You had no idea what that could've done," Lenny scolded.

"I've long since said goodbye to giving a shit about worst-case scenarios. Start talking, chubby."

C H . 4 2
IT'S   HARD
TO   BE   ALPHA

We didn't notice that the craft had begun the docking process when we were threatening Lenny's life. Before Lenny could say a word, the transport's doors opened up to enormous docking bay. Ships of varying similarity were lined up in rows and columns as far as I could see, enough of them to slightly make anyone nauseous.

"Kansas?" Drake guessed.

"Welcome to the rebellion," Lenny proudly announced as he confidently exited the craft.

He ignored our current promise of death, contingent on our hunger for information we probably couldn't understand being sated. Lenny continued for a few more steps, then turned back to us.

"You can kill me later. For now, let me show you why I was looking for you."

He led us to a chamber of pure light and energy. The closer we got, the more I felt like I knew what it was to touch the sun. The intensity slowed our pace, but Lenny walked right through. A few seconds later, we joined him. Inside was a room of count-less panels, all showing videos or massive amounts of scrolling data. "And this is Alpha."

"What is this? Where are we? Are we—" I fired off a series of questions before Lenny interrupted with an answer that read my mind.

"In an Employer base? Yes and no. It was. And then we took it over."

"Who is 'we'? What is the rebellion? Rebellion against what?"

"The Employers. We have found a way to fight back. We are hunting them."

"Who is 'we'?"

"Heroes, like us."

"We're no heroes, chubby," Drake corrected.

"Depends on what side of the war you are standing on."

"What war?" I asked.

"Us against them. The Employers. We are taking the fight to them."

Lenny selected several panels that displayed video feeds of various settings. "This is who we are."

"All teams, this is Alpha. Mission is green. I repeat: mission is green," Lenny announced to the selected panels.

The feeds exploded with activity. Each selected panel jostled forward, making it seem each feed was attached to a person.

The centermost panel displayed a frozen tundra, nothing but snow and ice blending into sky.

The second panel looked down the rusty circular stairwell of a tall tower. Light shot in from the many small, square holes that lined the tower, but could only do so much to show just how far down the stairwell went before being lost in darkness.

The third and fourth panels showed a strawberry field by the moonlight, while the last panel Lenny selected showed a rather large hospital. Even though the third and fourth panels were moving in the same manner as the first two, the fifth one looked like a simple traffic cam feed.

"What's going on, chubby?" Drake demanded.

"We are assaulting several suspected Employer assault teams

hunting heroes like us," Lenny answered. He knew we were there, but he was so engaged in monitoring the otherwise boring feeds that we could've been worlds away.

"You keep saying we, us. I mean, heroes, yeah, I got it, but do you all have a name, maybe?" I stumbled my way to a question.

I was still struggling to piece together what we were experiencing. The weakest of us standing stronger than I bet he had ever imagined. Shit, he was commanding others. Where could he have gone in such a short time to become so different? It was intoxicating. The longer we stood there with him, the more I felt like hope was returning to my thoughts, challenging the constant internal, drumming damnation of this all, the question of why I must be involved with it at all, as opposed to the blissfully ignorant normals that made up the rest of humanity.

"No."

"You wanna be a little more descriptive, big guy?" I urged.

"Shh!" Lenny harshly silenced.

His concentration was solely on the five hovering panels. It was like he was there in each setting. If anything, we were probably nothing more than errant voices in his head to be ignored.

All the video feeds stopped moving. All five panels' views rotated to capture the entire surroundings.

Lenny led two fingers two his temple, then nodded in confirmation. "Move in," he whispered.

The first panel moved several feet forward, but then was met by a maelstrom of plasma rounds. The feed continued on, but ceased moving. It stayed fixed on a downward angle toward the ground, bringing a look of complete horror on Lenny's face. After that, everything went to shit.

The strawberry fields met a similar fate as those in the frozen tundra. The tower and hospital showed something different, but no less harrowing. In both screens, the Alt descended upon the scene like dark shrouds.

"No." Lenny began to shake his head. "No, no, no. Talk to me. Team Echo. Foxtrot. Talk to me!"

This is Foxtrot. Things are bad. Hold on, a voice said, though I wasn't sure where it came from. I wasn't even sure if I heard it, but more felt the words articulated in my thoughts.

"You hear that?" Drake said, looking at me.

The fifth panel zoomed to the rooftop of the hospital, just as it was beginning to focus on a white-cloaked figure approaching the Alt that showed up when Lenny's attack began. The feed caught a hero jumping off the roof while shooting back at the figure. Following him came two more heroes, gunning at the first.

We got a party crasher. Some asshole showed up just before the Alt and attacked us. I'm sorry. We took out half of the hospital. But we will make it up by bringing this hero to you. Hold on—doesn't appear to be in league with the Alt. This could get ugly. Stand by.

"I'm hearing voices, Lenny," I finally had to ask.

"Not now," Lenny hushed.

"No, fat boy. Now," Drake said as he went to threaten Lenny with his gun.

Lenny, refusing to have his attention deterred, and sensing Drake's violent tendencies, quickly blocked Drake's attempt and brought his gun up to Drake's head. It wasn't until he felt my weapon against his head he reconsidered his ability to help his team if he were dead.

"Talk," I said coldly.

"Really? Like, 'take your weapon away from my buddy's head' is not the first thing you say?" Drake mockingly questioned.

"Goddammit!" Lenny shouted.

"Talk, fatty," Drake said as he slowly but firmly relinquished Lenny from his weapon.

"I don't have time for this shit. They need me!" Lenny screeched.

"What's going on?" I demanded.

"I told you!"

"You didn't tell us shit. Fuck why, how about you start with how we're here, and then tell us what the fuck is going on," Drake ordered.

"Fuck!" Lenny screamed. "Fine. Back at the elementary school, when you dicks kept shooting me and yelling at me. Remember? Yeah, well the fucking Alt came. There I was, just me—with weakened goddamn activeskin."

He took a moment to leer at Drake before continuing on.

"I was fucking dead. I was alone. You two always had each other's back, but never mine. Yeah, I sucked at battle, but without me, you two dicks would've been wiped out in Massachusetts."

"Bold statement from someone who experienced his first battle in a trunk," Drake challenged.

"You assholes put me in there!"

At this point, the second panel was alive with weapon fire. Whatever force Lenny had in the tower was outgunned ten to one. The fifth panel had given up their chase of the mysterious intervening hero, and focused on the Alt bearing down on them.

Gonna need evac, Alpha, Foxtrot announced.

Lenny once again placed two fingers against his temple and said, "Negative, Team Foxtrot. No evacs are available. Continue to strategically retreat. Sensors show there doesn't appear to be backup on the way for the Alt. Your failsafe exit is still open."

"Doesn't look good, chubby. Failsafe is always a euphemism for 'pretty much fucked.' Better tell us what's going on. Maybe we can help," Drake said.

"Fuck you. Fuck you. That is why you are here. But instead of letting me direct my teams, you keep asking the same fucking question. Fuck. You. There's your answer."

Lenny's outburst barely preceded all but the fifth panel going to static, presumably from cut feeds.

"Talk to us, Lenny."

"The Alt were going to kill me, no thanks to my 'friends'. Then a group of heroes came out of nowhere and wiped them all out. They were about to kill me, but one of them stopped the group and took me with them. I've been with them ever since. You won't believe where I've been."

"Speed up to when I give a fuck. How are you running military strikes from the belly of the beast?" Drake snapped.

The thought made Lenny chuckle.

"Something funny, fatty?"

"This is no belly, my friend. This is one base. This beast is much larger than you could imagine."

"Fuck it, I say kill him," Drake said as he cocked his battle-shotgun.

"Why were they looking for us, Lenny?" I asked.

"You didn't see it? We are good, but we just got slaughtered out there. We can find heroes, sure. There's more of us than you think. But to turn this thing, to have a chance, we don't need any more heroes like me. My power is here, operationally, but I'm no killer. Not if I have my way. Most out there aren't, either. Most of them are alive mainly from luck. We are using them because we haven't got much left, and those gifted enough to survive that fight are dying off as we lose this war. We need more like you two. We need those that will lust for the kill and pull off the impossible to satisfy it."

"Wars don't get won with the addition of two people."

"But it could be lost without them," Lenny corrected.

C H . 4 3
BETTER TO BE THE BEAR THAN GOLDILOCKS

An alarm rang out, filling the station with loud, foghorn sounds and black lights. Lenny's face contorted to pure sorrow. Something was beyond wrong.

Alpha, Silverstein is down. We need evac, now! was the last thing we all heard before the data chamber shattered around us into flaring electrical particles that dissolved into absolute nothingness.

"They found us," Lenny said as he rushed to the other side of the chamber to look down a hallway.

"Found us? You said this was an Employer base," I challenged.

"It was. It is. I need to think," Lenny said while holding his head. It looked like he was trying to mentally run away.

"Too late for that, fatty," Drake said, joining Lenny to peer down the hallway. "We in the shit together, or not? You tell us what the fuck is going on, right now, right here, or I'll fucking end you now so I don't have to worry about my back when whatever the fuck is coming gets here. Talk!"

"I failed them...all of them.... They're all dead...because of me."

On the other end came what concerned Lenny so much.

"Come on, Lenny. We've handled worse than that," Drake started.

"Shit, just the other day—"

"No! You don't get it. The ones that hunt me aren't like the others. They don't fight fair."

"They look like regular Alt to me," I said. I eased my way in between the corner of the doorway and where Lenny was standing, considering it was clear he wasn't going to be raising a weapon anytime soon.

Without looking, pained, Lenny responded, "They're not."

There were only five of them. No bigger, badder, or meaner than any other Alt Drake and I had faced. However, I could've sworn the light dampened around them.

When the Alt got within a hundred yards or so, they abruptly stopped. The leader took a step forward and observed his surroundings before nodding to himself and turning to his fellow Alt. They all nodded, nonchalantly and reversed their direction, disappearing around the corner.

"Umm..." I began.

"That doesn't feel right," Drake added.

The entire station began to shake something awful. Then a flash of intense light and heat, followed by a series of explosions, ripped away the outer walls of the hallway, section by section. Howling winds rushed in from the air outside, making it impossible to hear Lenny try hurry past us in an attempt to get to the hallway to the hanger bay.

Unfortunately for Lenny, he miscalculated the force of the gravitational pull from the exposed, crumbling section of the station and was swept away on the falling section.

Drake began to laugh uncontrollably at the sight as if he had lost his mind altogether. He continued to hysterically laugh for a few more seconds before looking up at me with tears of complete joy.

"Call me fucking nuts, but I just have this feeling that he

doesn't have to die this way," Drake proclaimed. When he was done speaking, his face went dead serious. He gave me the same look he gave me when the Battles begun. He pierced my soul to see what measure of courage it had, to see if I could match his insanity and lust for the impossible.

Not saying another word, Drake retreated back several paces, then raced off the crumbling station along with some of the debris. Every second he was in my sight felt like a year. I couldn't help but marvel at how much I agreed with him. I raced off after.

The sky was the type of biting cold that teased at hypothermia in odd areas and made your own lungs betray you in the simple act of trying to breathe without burning. A few seconds later, I began to see everything different.

Gravity was no longer one-directional. I began to see pieces of the falling station as a climbing wall that was beneath me, opposed to in front of me. There was no up, there was no down. There were simply places to go.

Travelling through the debris like an obstacle course, I finally found Drake, who had caught up to poor Lenny. Drake couldn't even meet my gaze while he looked at our friend who was frozen in animation. The strained look on Lenny's face suggested his heart exploded. He never had a chance.

Everything on Earth was getting bigger now as we raced back toward it. I hadn't a clue what the plan was to survive this, but I also couldn't shake the fact that I also hadn't a worry about it.

Drake finally snapped to and peered over the ledge to see how close we were. Waiting a few seconds, he held up his two fists. He began to count down with one hand. Once he got to zero, he made a thumbs-up with his other hand and started pumping upward.

Both of us jumped just as the impact from the landing shot us back towards the sky some hundred feet. Instead of going splat, we somehow landed on desert dunes and kept running.

Running from the rain shower of a destroyed cloud station. Running from the Alt that brought it down. Running from the improbability of surviving. We just ran until all I could remember was face-planting into a dune, hoping that my sleep would be nothing short of eternal.

C H . 4 4
CAN'T SPARE NATASA

New Mexico, 2007

Getting tired of leaning against the wall, Sunday moved past me and sat down on Serrick's slowly decomposing body. She motioned for me to join her, but I passed.

"I'm good," I waved off.

"Well, you're not dead."

"Guess not."

"Do you think he is dead?"

"Lenny? Yeah."

"How can you be so sure?"

"I can't. I guess that's becoming the point; I can't be sure of anything."

"What do you mean?"

"Multiple dimensions within people not enough?"

"You don't have to accept what I've told you, nor even what you yourself have experienced, for that matter."

"No, I do. What do I have left? All else has been stripped away. Day by day, battle by battle. I can't deny what I have seen any more than I can this conversation. I really can't doubt anything you have said or have done. But the thing that still kicks me in the nuts every time I try to believe in your intentions is that I am reminded of one unnerving thing: I still don't know why you are telling me this."

"I told you—"

"No, I get it. You don't want us—rather, Drake—to kill a hero you think Samytus wants dead for the Employers. But if that's the case, why are you telling me? If you really have watched our battles together, you would definitely know neither I, nor anyone, is his fucking handler. That soldier marches to his own drumbeat."

"You shield him."

"Oh, for fuck's sake…." I rolled my eyes. "What does that mean?"

"Really, I don't even know if there is a specific term for it. I just know, or have seen, that since you two have gotten together, you behave like symbiotic parasites in a relationship that has the potential for mass destruction. Somehow, when you are around him, no one can see the fact that he is obviously a Relevant powerful enough to be ignorant of his own powers. He only releases it when you subconsciously want him to."

I'd had enough. Slow down time, speed it up, send me to hell or a planet like it, I could give a shit. I was done. My mind had given up on achieving some sort of internal combustion to cleanse myself of all this. Now I controlled a sociopath that happened to be my only friend thanks to brutal survival?

Fuck it.

"The bar wasn't my handiwork," Sunday added. "I just took advantage of some hero's powerful slip."

"You're lying," was all I could think or say.

"Somewhere in that beautifully dysfunctional rat's nest you call a mind, you must know that I have no reason to lie to you. If you have been listening to me, then you of course remember that I have multiple resources at my disposable. Toying with you for the fuck of it, though fun, would just be a waste of my time. Don't flatter yourself. It's slowing us down." Sunday shut me down.

"Insulting me would be exactly what I would do to disarm

me."

"Or fucking killing you, but you know, I'm weighing my options."

"So what? Are you trying to get me to think I need to kill Drake instead?"

"If I told you I didn't know, would you believe the next thing I said after that, or anything I have said before?"

"I'm not sure what I believe now."

"Then the point is perspective. I could be wrong a thousand ways, and we wouldn't even feel a breeze from the wind of change that wiped us away from memory. But if I'm right, we won't be depriving ourselves of the possibility of the sweet revenge we all deserve for being put in this situation. There are more out there to kill to make this right. Samytus. The Employers. No, we have far more work to do than ending it all with one cheap kill."

"Should we fight?"

"Why wouldn't we?"

"Because we have turned into monsters, by fate or design. Because in our path towards justice, we have done exactly what the Employers have done. Aren't we worse? Shouldn't we be stopped?"

"Ask yourself that question."

"I haven't stopped since you told me the Employers designed all this for us poor fucks to hunt down and kill gods of creation in other dimensions. We...I have killed civilizations by the dozens with fewer than fifty bodies to show for it."

I couldn't stand anymore. The sickening pit in my stomach finally buckled my knees, drove me against the wall and down to the floor in an emotional mess. I wasn't sure if I could do it anymore. I had no right.

"Because fuck Samytus, that's why," Sunday said. "Because this has to end somewhere. Because each new day, I lose touch with knowing what it was like to be mortal, and that is frightening. Because if this is my fate, then I have no choice. Neither do you."

Suddenly, the thought of my sister came to mind. She was more like a mother, even with having the best parents anyone could ask for. She would laud over me, protect me when I didn't need it, speak for me when I had my own thoughts, fight for me when I was perfectly happy to surrender. She loved me like a possession.

The thoughts drove pangs of anguish through my heart. In that moment, I yearned to be dead, just to escape the heartache thinking of my sister brought. I felt her last moments; her fear, her pain. I couldn't breathe. I grabbed at my chest, but felt nothing, as if I didn't exist. I felt nothing, then saw nothing.

It only lasted moments before everything came back and Sunday was in midsentence about how she began tracing heroes back to worlds similar to Lenny's after the fall.

"While you two were passed out," she continued, "all my searches pointed to well-recorded history of the collapse of all of Lenny's dimensions once he supposedly died from the fall. Every civilization connected to Lenny's dimensions spoke of the violent and sudden removal of all Lenny's influences in the matter of a breath. However, soon after, heroes bearing resemblances to those of Lenny's dimensions appeared in dimensions that once celebrated the presence of Alpha. But these Alpha heroes weren't there to be those dimensions' heroes. While those new ones conquered, I traced them back to a dimension that existed in the space-time where Lenny's dimensions once existed.

"Salt. Not only is Lenny still alive, he has wanted you and Drake dead from the start."

Memories of Lenny and Drake's conversation in the Common came storming back. Even with tacitly believing Sunday that Lenny secretly guided us from battle to battle, it was a whole other thing to accept that Lenny was only keeping us close so he could kill us.

Sunday was still talking, and I did my best to listen, but I was caught in the fact that Lenny always seemed to know a little too much. How he oddly could be the most calm of the three of us while simultaneously pissing his pants. I continued to miss everything she said until "Natasa."

I snapped out of it. "What was that?"

"What part?"

"What you just said. That name. Say it again. Name for what?"

"What? The newly discovered dimension where all the new heroes were coming from?"

"Yeah, whatever. The name!"

"Natasa. The dimension's name is the Natasa Contingency System. It's where those assholes you ran into after passing out in the dunes are from. I think Lenny created it, and retreated to there during the fall."

I did everything possible to ignore the name of Lenny's new dimension, or why he would ever know that name. I never spoke of my family with him, or anyone.

"What about his body?" I asked.

"The only time I've seen something similar is when the soul believed to be dying isn't actually from this dimension. But generally that's done by a rare type of Recluse, and is done by sacrificing his or her place in that dimension. Returning to the 'dead body' would result in complete dimensional collapse."

Ch . 4 5
But Enemies of Enemies Make Strange Bedmates

Nevada, 2006

"Hey. Hey. Cholahk phucked up, mahn. Chorite? Chorite?"

I opened my eyes, fully expecting to be dead. Almost daring God to open my eyes to sunlight. The anticipation of final judgment was crushing. Finding a toothless bum standing over me, given a halo by the high noon desert sun, contradicted the depths of hell or (dare I say it) the Pearly Gates I was expecting. "Surprised" just isn't a strong enough word to describe the feeling I fought as I began to sit up. Never mind the fact I had no fucking clue what this guy was saying. Perhaps the awkward, gangly, light-skinned black kid with freckles standing curiously next to him could walk me through it.

"He asked if you were alright," the kid finally said before he and the bum pointed battleautomatics at us.

"Fuck me, he speaks?" Drake asked, rising to a sitting position about ten feet away.

He, like me and my two new friends, was in a metallic and plastic forest formed by the falling station. I wasn't sure which miracle to focus on—surviving the fall or not getting crushed by debris. It felt easier to focus on the kid and the bum holding hero weapons to our heads.

"Whoa there, freckles. Get to know us first before you hate us."

"You're heroes. I fucking hate heroes," the tall kid responded.

"Hey. Slappy," Drake began to offer. "We're not too fond of them either. We kill them, you know."

"Fuck you. That's all you do. But for right now, the only thing I need to know is whose hero will you become?"

"Now you know, WeaponsJesus—that's why I've been keeping this boy alive," said a voice that drew yet more hatred from the kid's face. "He's useful! Look what he found us."

Turning to see who was new to this little party of ours, I saw five men. Each looked like he had just been kicked off the set of any post-apocalyptic nuclear holocaust movie destined for late-night cable. The leader—the voice—stood in the middle.

Long, scraggly brown hair dangled past his tanned face and salt-and-pepper goatee. His body was strong, but had the type of muscularity that came from a life of hardened labor rather than lifting weights. His upper torso was covered only by a tattered and worn flak jacket. His outfit was completed with camouflage pants tucked into Doc Martins and held up by a punk rocker's studded belt.

"You boys fell into the wrong part of the country," he said through a shit-eating grin that accompanied his aviator shades—no doubt ripped from a dead policemen's body.

"No, no, no, the village people should never be allowed to hold weapons," Drake cut in.

"Careful, son. You just got a knife in this here gunfight."

"This here…yeah, yeah. I'm the dick that brings a knife to a gunfight and wins," Drake returned as he held up one of his battlebraces and marveled at his constant companions.

"The fuck…?" I whispered.

"What?" Drake asked casually.

"You steal that?" I asked, turning my attention completely to Drake as if we didn't have multiple weapons aimed at our person.

"Steal what?" Drake asked with a forced innocence.

"You fucking hack. You stole that phrase. The phrase. The fucking 'I'm the guy who brings a knife to a gunfight' shit. You stole it from that fucking bartender that pulled the shotgun on us."

"Naw."

"Yeah, you did, you fucking hack. You got that shit from the bartender."

"Naw, I said that. I said that back in Connecticut or some shit."

"You got that from the fucking bartender in Tennessee. Fucking hack."

"Well, even if I did, I don't think he will miss it."

"Hey! Think we had the floor, here," said the post-apocalyptic leader.

"Who the fuck are you, and why do you think I give a fuck?" I asked, growing more and more tired of humoring the situation at all.

"Fuck off, Moses," the tall kid said in a tired voice.

"Easy, junior," Moses, the presumed leader, said. "Play your cards right, and you might walk out of this one. You know I don't like killing softbacks."

"Normals!"

"Whatever stops the tears, sweetie,"

"What makes you think accepting death is an unacceptable fate?" the kid said coolly. He moved one of his battleautomatics from us to aim at Moses.

The men standing behind Moses brandished hero weapons as well. In the cruel glare of the sun, the guns looked ten times their normal size. At this point in the conversation, Drake and I had two battlerifles, three battleautomatics, and two battleshotguns aimed at us.

"Allow me to introduce ourselves," Moses politely stated,

taking cue from the distinct sound of hero weapons being drawn. "The gentle-looking man to my far right, with the two battleshotguns, is WeaponsJesus."

"The men to my immediate left and right are MohomedDA-SuicideKING and NegativeGhadi, respectively. And to my far left, HolyADAMbomb. I am Moses420. Together, we control this region under the name of the Five Fingers of God!"

Moses posed with dramatic flair.

"You believe this shit? Ah, man that's corny!" The kid spat at Moses.

"WeaponsJesus, what's this look like to you?" Moses asked, turning his head slightly to address his compadre.

"Dirty holy rumba," the little man grumbled in a distinct accent that was worlds away from the pronunciation of his name stereotypically suggested.

"That's right, WJ—Mexican standoff."

Great! Think the end of the movie Face/Off, where everyone in the church had a gun on someone they wanted to shoot, and doves—so many doves. We all had someone we wanted to shoot. Sadly, we were without weapons. It was a travesty that we didn't have any doves.

Another thing that betters your chances is to be in a team of like-minded people, who are also armed, and don't want you dead. Now, I was cool with Tongueless George over there. One, he appeared to be the only person not aiming a gun at us. And two, I think we bonded when he stared me into waking up. Whether his name was Tongueless George or not was irrelevant.

Freckles, however, had some animosity that made me think he didn't want me to live anymore. At the very least, he hated me for reasons beyond me. Strangely, I understood the hatred, if not the reasons.

"Last chance, Billy," Moses said once he was done posing.

"Did I stutter when I said fuck off?" the kid returned. "And who the fuck is Billy?"

"I'll give him this: he's got balls," Drake admitted.

"Now, now, Billy," Moses said in an exhausted yet enthusiastic voice. "Don't start this again. And we were doing so well. You know why I call you that? It's because you're too white to be a Jamal."

"Fuck you," the kid snapped, clearly not cool with being told what he was.

"Though I applaud the exuberant response…" Moses began again.

"¡Euforico!" WJ suddenly shouted.

"Thank you, WJ," Moses said with a general air of acceptance.

"What is he? Your yes man?" I asked, pointing toward the troll of a man with long, unkempt hair naturally woven into Rasta-worthy dreads.

WJ may have been six feet once, but a lifetime of criminal hunching probably reformed his spine into a nice "c" shape, leaving him standing around a cool four-foot-two. Very commanding. Scary to think his weapon of choice was the battleshotgun—let alone two of them.

Turning his attention back to Billy and my side of the sandbox, Moses continued, "Still, the response was not necessary. No time for a thin hide, boy. Listen, it's quite simple. You can't be a Jamal. Am I right, fellas?"

He half-heartedly turned to his crew with his arms out, pausing to observe their obedient nods. This was not to actually witness their agreement; it was becoming painfully clear that at this level of sheep to shepherd, Moses could feel the compliance of the flock.

"Now, I was wrapping my head around it all night after I first met you, and something just didn't sit right. I mean, here's this tall, handsome, redheaded stepchild coming toward me with the cutest set of freckles anyone this side of Appalachia has seen, and he ruins it by announcing that his name is Jamal. Now, if that don't make a dick hair's wig, I don't know what does. Now, his—"

"What the fuck does a 'dick hair's wig' mean?" Drake asked.

"No sense, boy. Now come, let ole Moses lead you to the right path. As I was saying—he then tells me that his full name is Jamal J. Williams, and dawn broke over Marblehead, you see. Well, hell, you take the 's' off his surname there, apply the friendly nickname that goes along with William—Billy—and there you have it."

Moses paused and posed, awaiting grand acceptance of his brilliance.

"And you got the name 'Moses' because...?" I asked, breaking his silent celebration.

"I don't know. That's for me and God to sort out," Moses replied nonchalantly. "Kill 'em."

In the momentary blue spark from a gun being fired, I saw coming over the heat-soaked horizon a convoy consisting of two open-faced transports racing toward us. I didn't need to see their uniforms to know the Alt were about to crash the party.

The impact from the sporadic rounds brought me back to the moment at hand. After falling from the sky, the weapon fire didn't hold the same rank on my list of most painful experiences, but I still withstood multiple impacts.

Taking advantage of his intent focus on the kid, I moved just under NegativeGhadi and launched myself, and a battlebrace in the form of a long, jagged sword, upward. The blade bisected him, with each half falling limp to the ground.

Drake took my lead, but was cut off and sent flying backward by the sudden impact of a transport's plasma round exploding near his feet.

The Alt had arrived, coming under a hailstorm of fire. It was a magnificent sight, them deftly deploying from the transport in a ghostly progression. Their shots steady and deliberate, WeaponsJesus and HolyADAMbomb stood and fell in vain defiance.

Not seeing wisdom in standing ground, Drake and I took off through the fallen debris. Running through the ruins of the destroyed suborbital station, we soon cleared the region of debris and found an open road leading us out. I heard a hollow wind coming closer and closer, as if the air before me was being sucked from behind.

It was one of the open-rig transports. It was a type I had never seen before, nor remembered Lenny talking about. The front resembled the cockpit of a stealth bomber-turned-skiff-jet, with the entire top ripped off and the body angled so the nose aimed down. Inside, the pilot's console rested in the middle, elevated from the rest of the craft, with enough room to let approximately ten Alt take offensive positions.

Standing in front of us was the tall, skinny kid and a BSR, who was waiting like a patient expert. He stood holding his breath, gun aimed. With an exhale, he fired two shots straight past our heads and into the pilot's eyes. The transport spun out of control, crashing into a nosediving barrel roll just in front of our faces. Bodies and machine parts were flung down the vacant, decrepit street until all rested in a bloody conclusion.

Finishing this masterpiece, Tongueless George appeared from a nearby rooftop, exposing a devastational cube and launching rockets into the crash site until the clicks of his empty chamber echoed through the dead streets. He then disappeared behind the house he was standing on.

"Fuck you if you think I'm thanking you," I said as my battlebraces began to form.

Tongueless George reappeared in a beaten SUV makeshifted into an open-top truck with roll bars.

"Come with me," Jamal calmly ordered.

C H . 4 6
I INVITE YOU

"Holy shit!" I exclaimed as we got in.

"Goddamn, that was close. You boys know how to make an entrance," Drake added as he sat back and relaxed, fully knowing his new companions were unknown and untrusted. His battlebraces continued to glow at the ready.

Seated between Drake and I was a twin of Jamal. Giving them both a second glance, I asked, "Which one of you hates heroes?"

"What do you mean?" Jamal growled from shotgun.

"Before those five dicks and a shitload of Alt showed up, one of you..." I said, pointing back and forth him and the twin, "wanted us dead. Then you save us. The way I figure it—"

"No one gives a fuck what you think. I'm doing this because I'm getting paid to."

"You three are fucking mercs?" Drake howled in a joyous roar. He could hardly contain himself as he doubled over in laughter.

"You better get your boy in control," Jamal warned.

"You get him in control. You're so good. Let's see how you do against a sociopath with alien shielding," I teased.

I was beginning to feel at ease with the threat of death in the same way Drake always seemed to be. It wasn't that I didn't believe the normal was able to kill both of us; it was that I cared less about facing that final moment when those who believe they still have a soul hesitate. There was power there, real power, and the more I escaped death by spitting in its face, the more I craved it.

"What's going on, freckles?" I asked, snapping Jamal out of the deep thought he sunk into while contemplating his future if he did in fact try to get Drake under control.

"My mother named me Jamal."

"Fair enough. I'm Salt. The one over there is Drake."

"I know who you are."

"Of course you do. This your brother?"

"Jayson," Jamal answered after dropping his eyes for a moment.

We suddenly veered off the road and began racing into the desert dunes.

"He doesn't talk? Like your friend here?" I asked while pointing to good ole Tongueless George, dutifully driving.

"He doesn't talk because of drugs." Jamal nodded toward the driver. "There was a time ole George here was the most feared drug dealer in this entire desert. Then, he was force-fed enough shrooms choke a cow by a rival gang. He tripped his mind out and wandered into the desert. A year later, he comes back looking gaunt, permanently dirty, and with a chewed-off tongue he displays proudly.

"My brother doesn't speak because of fucks like you."

"What's your connection to George?"

"My brother worked for him. I hated it. I hated George. I hated my brother more. But when whatever responsible for you fucking heroes arrived to our sleepy little town and a battle broke out on our doorstep, George and my brother were all I had left. I'll kill them when I'm done killing all of you."

That comment was met with a smile and an approving nod from Tongueless George. Jayson, Jamal's twin, sat motionless. I wasn't sure if he couldn't talk because of something physical like George, or from the refusal to open his mouth, or to avoid diverting energy from whatever he was concentrating on.

"What's keeping you from killing them now?"

"I promised my mother I wouldn't. It's the only thing I can remember her saying. It's the only way to hear her voice. I can't until I've avenged her, or until I can remember her saying anything else. Anything."

"We all have our curse, don't we?"

"Is that what we are doing here? You taking us to the slaughterhouse?" Drake cut in.

"Your dance is promised to another," Jamal answered. "I only got paid to get you there. I don't know what the plans are for you. Don't give a shit."

"Mind telling us who you are doing this for? Sorry, who paid you to retrieve us?"

"No."

"Oh, fuck no, this isn't going to work." Drake began to shake his head, looking down. He then snapped a battlebrace into a blade and laid it across his lap, barely avoiding seeringJayson's lap. "This won't do."

"Whoa, whoa, whoa," I said after leaning in to try to halt the possible bloodshed, and subsequent vehicle accident. "What's with the secrecy? Why won't you tell us?"

"Not part of the contract," Jamal replied coldly. He didn't even bother to turn his head as he continued to stare forward.

"Is keeping that part of your contract worth your life?"

"It is if I don't plan on dying."

CH. 47
DON'T GET
TO CHOOSE

A dull hiss could be heard, followed by a loud crack, like the air ignited. The silhouette of the transports we escaped could be seen on the horizon, but now accompanied with several more.

"Here we go," Jamal said, acknowledging what I saw wasn't a mirage.

He reached down and retrieved the BSR he held before, secretly wedged between the driver's seat and me. He stood up to take aim.

"Think you're going to need something bigger than that, freckles," Drake warned.

"It's all we got."

"The fuck...?" Drake started as he sized the kid up again.

Knowing Drake, he was rethinking how good this normal might actually be if he was getting paid to tumble with heroes and only carried a sniper rifle. If anything, the kid's willingness to be in dire situations to achieve the impossible for ultimate success impressed him, but that only took the kid so far.

"How many?" Drake asked.

"How many what?"

"How many you kill before heroes began using you for their

dirty work?"

"Who said it was a hero?"

"Your disdain for using a talent for something you hate."

"Every dead hero is a good one for me. Doesn't matter if I get paid for it or not."

Jamal fired off two shots. Nothing happened, and the silhouettes grew larger.

"You really think we won't kill you?" I asked.

"I think that wouldn't be in your best interest right now."

"What about when we get to where you want to take us, or at least, escape our current predicament?"

"Guess I'm just hoping my death wish isn't granted today," Jamal answered before firing off two more shots, still appearing to hit nothing.

"Fine," I said, choosing to go at the spiteful teen another way. "Why with them? I mean, I get that you seem to be some Bruce Wayne in the making, but why the mutes?"

Jamal fired two more shots. Then two more. Then he emptied the clip, before reaching down to reload the BSR. He fired another two shots before saying another word.

"They talk to each other," he began. "It happened sometime after I promised my mother. Jayson wasn't injured in the battle that killed our mother. He was injured several battles prior. He was caught in a blast."

Jamal let out a chuckle, and then two more shots before going on.

"Funny part is he should've been evaporated from the blast, but something completely shielded him except a thin metal sliver that passed through his temples. He hasn't spoken since. Our mother was the only one who could communicate with him. When you heroes took her, too, George began subconsciously moving to my brother's thoughts. I didn't know until he led me to the one who hired me to find you."

CH. 48
NO REST FOR THE WICKED

Jamal continued to fire in two-shot successions until he needed to reload another clip.

"You are a horrible shot," Drake informed him.

"Not trying to kill them," Jamal answered, unnerved from Drake's criticism.

"Then why waste the rounds?"

"Trying to slow them down."

"For what?"

"Look ahead."

We followed Jamal's direction. Beyond the dust kicking up from our violent speed was the image of more ruins. These were more clay and traditional, like those of most small buildings and houses in the southwest United States.

"What is this place?" I asked.

"Some of your fucking handiwork. The station you took down wasn't the first. Most of the time, the debris falls out in the middle of nowhere, but this village where you two landed wasn't so lucky."

The transports were now close enough to make out details. Each of the five racing towards us held about ten Alt. Running through ruins wasn't going to do it. I gave Drake a look to convey that I had no faith in our current plan, and he jumped up.

"Gimme that goddamn thing," Drake barked as he snatched the BSR out of Jamal's hands. "The best defense is killing every last one of them."

Drake sat down in between the driver and passenger seats, facing the transports. He didn't squint or hold his breath. No, he took in a deep drag from the blunt he was chewing down to a small, lit nub, and let out a barrage of shots.

The second transport from the right nosedived into fantastic tumbling explosion, but the other four broke formation and increased speed. Drake kept firing, but it appeared that they could adapt as fast as he could pull the trigger. Each foot we traveled, they gained ten. They were gonna be on us far before we had a chance to reach the ruins.

No part of me felt like any of this was going to work. Drake didn't miss; he toyed with his prey. But now, this detachment of Alt dodged him like they knew exactly where he wanted to fire and simply moved slightly aside. One transport sped forward and took the lead of the group.

"It's not working," I whispered.

"Easy, muffin. You just let Daddy handle the monsters in the closet," Drake coolly responded, firing three more shots. "Clip."

"Last one," Jamal stated, just as coolly. He handed Drake the clip.

"Of fucking course," Drake said, reaching back without breaking his gaze.

"It's not working," I repeated.

"Salt," Drake cautioned.

The lead transport bucked forward, increasing space between it and the rest of the group. As it got even closer to us, the rest moved into a single-file formation, increasing their speed in the process.

"It's not working."

"Salt."

"It's not working."

"Salt. Salt. Salt."

It didn't matter. I was fixated on the probability of the worst outcome. Our chances in these situations had always danced on the line between impossible and no chance in hell. But even from the first battle, Drake and I attacked the impossible as if there were no other way to approach it. This wasn't that. This, our choice of strategy, wasn't going to work.

"Salt!" I heard Drake's yell. It pulled at my attention, but quickly disintegrated into background information.

I don't remember leaping from the SUV, just the warmth my body felt when traveling through the desert air. It was the closest to euphoria I think I will ever get. I felt the presence of God for the first time, or something as great. It was bliss, and then came the brimstone.

My battlebrace met the nose of the lead transport as my feet landed cleanly on its tip with the weight of elephants, sending it crashing to the ground. While the tumbling transport was caught in real time, my perspective slowed down enough for me to run up the transport and slice through its cockpit. Once the transport was halved, I leapt through it and onto the next one.

The pilot of the transport was the first Alt I killed. I then worked my way through the rest, until our pilotless transport came to its logical, fiery barrel-rolling conclusion. I was too busy hacking blindly through the Alt to notice the danger of the crash. I was only saved by being sandwiched between multiple dead Alt.

I hauled myself out of that mangled mess just in time to see the other three transports circling back. The giant sandstorm that kicked up from their thrusters after turning around made it clear they were no longer fucking around.

Salvaging through the bodies, I grabbed a couple of battler-ifles and battleshotguns. I was about to set up an offensive position when it struck me—like Pulp Fiction's Butch choosing weapons—that I was thinking small. Giving it another go, I found my prize and emerged with a devastational-cube. After taking cover,

I stepped out and fired off every rocket the weapon had loaded.

The trail of light behind the five rockets was mesmerizing. I couldn't help but to follow them instead of their target, but luckily for me, my blind rage had a divine benefactor and guided most of them directly into a transport, with the last two racing through the explosion.

I waited for the first one to pass, but stepped out in front of the second and opened fire with the battlerifle. It should have been enough to only kill the pilot, maybe, but definitely not enough to stop the whole craft. It should have continued through me like brush on a track, hopefully ending my murderous mystery in the process. But oddly, the pilot veered away from me.

The craft struck the destroyed transport next to me and spun out of control. The pilot tried to right the craft, but it only resulted in the transport tipping on its side and flipping into a fantastic, explosive end. Just past them, on foot, came the rest of the Alt.

I took off toward the destroyed transport between us to get position on them. Right before I was about to fire, the closest Alt fell from a BSR round. Coming out of the dust storm like a Mad Max-sponsored cavalry was Drake and the rest.

Feeling even more invincible, I once again stepped out from cover. I began to feel what each Alt wanted to do next. Those furthest away were the easiest. I picked them off one by one, until it was just those who were close to begin with.

I also felt Drake's presence close by and tossed up the battleshotgun I had slung to my back. I followed that with a battlebrace through the upper chest of the closest Alt. Drake shot the next one as I ducked under and circled around a piece of the transport dug into the ground, until I could get to the Alt close to attacking Drake's back. Drake stepped and shot, I moved and impaled, until they were all dead.

Neither of us said anything until we were resting comfortably in the backseat of the SUV. As it pulled away, Drake looked to me and said, "That was a crazy fucking minute, huh?"

C H . 4 9
BOOK OF RAGE,
VERSE 36:72

California, 2006

After driving through the night in an SUV that seemed to have no need to refuel, we finally saw something other than the desert. The problem was the sight we saw was hard to accept.

"Correct me if I'm wrong," Drake began, "but—"

"There should be land here, not what sounds like the ocean," I cut in.

The horizon looked like it dropped off a cliff and disappeared into opaque greyish white clouds. We hadn't been on a road since leaving the adobe ruins, but fuck me if we weren't on a path. Everything was gone, but in its place was the commanding sound of the ocean slamming against land. Awe-aspiring sight, if horrifying. But the horror was made worse by the SUV approaching it at full speed.

"You going to tell ole TG to slow down?" I asked Jamal.

"Why? We aren't there yet."

I wanted to respond, but my stomach shooting to my throat prevented that when the car took a drastic dive, amazingly hugging the road. Nothing could be seen in, around, or through the fog as Tongueless George raced to our assured watery death.

Soon, I became so cold the air rushing into my lungs made it hard to breathe. Then came the sun and a view that pierced my soul: the clearest sky I had ever seen, over the most pristine blue ocean gently rippling around a monotone metropolis from a future beyond my imagination. Towers disappeared into the sky as the sun splashed rays off the gleaming buildings. With a touch more gold shimmer, I would have believed I was on my way to heaven. But's that is when I noticed we were traveling on a massive non-celestial bridge.

"I was told by the hero you are about to meet that this place was the result of an epic battle between you heroes and those you claim oppress you," Jamal said while giving a nod to the grand city. "Just looks like a lot of forgotten dead people at the hands of you selfish fucks to me. Welcome to NLA"

Ole TG continued to navigate with the same ease he did the desert, while Jayson remained silent with his head down. Jamal wasn't much for conversation, and Drake was knee-deep in convincing himself that what he was seeing wasn't the result of tripping balls while he was, in fact, currently tripping balls. Being a little bit of an anime fanboy myself, I was taking all the sights in.

Nothing made sense, but everything did at once. It should've been there; we shouldn't have been there. There should have been towns and cities in its place on the way to Los Angeles, if that was even where we were supposed to go. But no, there were futuristic structures throughout a sprawling, immaculately clean metropolis. Making matters worse for my perception of reality, all the people looked like they belonged in the time from before we entered the fog.

"Appleseed," an unknown voice said into my right ear.

Fighting every nerve I had to not automatically come up with an active battlebrace for fear I was tripping balls (considering I smoked some of what Drake did) and accidently impale Jayson in the head, I turned to see a man I had never seen before somehow sitting comfortably in between me and Jayson.

"That was his muse," the man continued to confide. "Serrick

Cross."

I could've asked him how he was there. Or how exactly he was sitting in a space between me and another person, but at least that was solved by noticing Jayson was no longer there. As for the other part—fuck it. Instead, I focused on the ominous "he" everyone keeps referring to and jumping through hoops for.

"I take it you work for the person responsible for all this, including hunting me and…." I stopped to check to see if Drake had even noticed the shift in our company. He had not.

"Can he see you?" I asked, pointing to Drake.

"The simplest answer is no," Serrick responded.

"There is another answer?"

"Multiple."

"Are you a figment of my imagination?"

"No."

"I guess the better question is would my figment of imagination be honest?"

"That depends on your soul, Hellokilla."

"Why did you call me that?"

"It's the name the person I am taking you to see prefers to call you by."

"You are taking me? Last I checked, ole TG was driving."

"Yes, that's right, Jamal…. Ole TG, as you call him, is driving. For security's sake, when we use contract help—especially normals—we like to make them believe they know who we are and are able to get to us. Gives them a sense of power. But no, it's just plain me."

Serrick was far from plain. If anything, he was the only thing that matched the futuristic setting. Platinum hair on top of a chiseled, yet genderless face. He wore a white-gray collarless suit to finish the look.

"And Jayson?"

"He is with the person I am taking you to see. We sort of switch places. I guide them to the location, and Jayson discusses mission details."

"You got to be shitting me. The mute calls the shots? What about his very protective brother who seems to think he is calling the shots?"

"Mentally at the same meeting, but having a different conversation."

"With the same person Jayson is physically speaking to?"

"Yes."

"And this is not a figment of my imagination?"

"Like you asked—would I be honest?"

"What about Drake?"

Serrick gave it a moment, as if he forgot the name Drake. Then he lit up and answered, "Ahh yes, MilitantRomeo. No, he thought it best to only speak with you."

"The person that has had my back since battle one wouldn't notice I was gone?"

Serrick gave it another hard thought to show he was sincerely searching for an answer before replying, "No."

C H . 5 0
JOLLY GOOD

My next thought came with me suddenly standing in a lush, sunken chamber that didn't know if it wanted to be Arabian Nights or The Fifth Element. Standing alone at the panoramic window wall in front of me was a man with long, curly brown hair and a tannish-white tunic.

Despite his Lemmy-style sideburns and mustache combination, he had a very soothing aura that wrapped itself around you, made you feel a sense of loyalty, and injected images of invincibility into one's thoughts. He didn't wave me over, or even say a word, but turning to face the view invited me.

Once I sidled up next to him, I could see what he saw. After a few seconds, I felt like I could hear the subtle hum of the busy streets below. Then the murmur of muddled conversations in a chorus of life. Then I began to feel that vast collection of life's emotion. All its joy, all its sorrow. It was crushing. That was when he decided to break the silence.

"Heavy is the head that wears the crown. Such a silly turn of a phrase, I always thought before the Battles. Now, standing here, I understand it. There is no justice without injustice, there are no heroes without monsters, there are no saints without sinners. There is just judgment," he said as he turned and extended his hand.

"Very nice to meet you, Hellokilla. I am Samytus Alltrue."

"Hero name?"

The question made him laugh, a bit off guard. He flashed a look of consideration, as if he hadn't thought about it before.

"No, funny enough. My hero name was Iraqi6ushm3n, or something or other. I've long since gone by my chosen name."

"Alltrue?"

Samytus continued to chuckle heartedly at the observations. Whether by act or circumstance, he was making it clear he was enjoying the interaction.

"I know, I know," he said, making a sheepish face with hands raised and turning side to side to add effect. "With all this…. The truth is, it's English."

"My name isn't Hellokilla."

"That all depends on where you are standing."

Turning back to look out the vast expanse of his view, Samytus changed the subject. "Breathtaking, isn't it? You should really see it at night. It is quite something. That is when things really get to work."

"How is this possible?"

"You see, the secret is in perception. Perception is key. I'm sure you've noticed the people walking around on the way here. They looked like they were from the time before our abductions, right? They are. And they think they have always lived in this setting. They have memories and work all rooted in the past, but charade'd by what they do now in the present. It doesn't. After they are done toiling about for the day and retire to their homes, that is when my utopian citizens come out to operate and maintain the city in shadow-like silence."

"None of your normals are night owls, huh?"

"Everyone sleeps by three a.m. Everyone awakes at eight a.m. The space and time in between belongs to my citizens of the night."

"No one remembers why they do or do not have to get up at eight a.m. every day?"

"It's called time-slippage. It happens when someone like me plays with reality. It affects everyone, but I've learned to create a myriad of time-slippages for all those who reside within this city. Everyone experiences the march of time a little different. Neighbor A might remember she was up since six a.m. watering her lawn, while Neighbor B believes he has been cycling around the city since waking up at five-thirty a.m." Both, however, have only been up for five minutes."

"Still haven't told me how is it possible for you to create a city in the space an entire landmass should be. Correct me if I'm wrong, but I crossed a bridge to get into this imaginary city."

"Does this feel imaginary to you?"

The anger that came from being asked that question was a sudden and violent rush that shocked me. I needed to read Samytus's face to know I reacted with more than shitty thoughts. Without looking down, I could see the glow from active battlebraces by my sides. Instead of attacking me, or even putting up a defense, Samytus simply turned and knelt on both knees with his head bowed.

"This isn't your imagination, Roman Salt. But what the Employers did to some of us has allowed for our imaginations to become reality. We are a chaotic, reckless, genocidal bunch that revels in our own ignorance towards the woe we reap. Killing me would only bring us closer to salvation."

"Is that why you brought me here—to kill you?"

"No, but part of the reason I need you is because you can. There were more like me, but unknowingly to your own consciousness, you and your friend systematically hunted each one of us down. I believe you are doing that because that is how the Employers told you this would end. I don't believe that, and I can prove it, but I need your help."

Something in the distance caught my eye. It was only a few tiny flashes at first, but then erupted into a brilliant series of explosions, leveling a whole city block in the process.

"They are getting close," Samytus softly announced.

CH. 51
REALIZING YOU ARE THE FOX AND NOT THE HOUND

The explosions were the result of a battle. Seeing that I wasn't in the mood for killing, Samytus got up and joined me at the window. Once he was next to me, the entire panoramic view was taken over by multiple images being rapidly moved into place. Soon, my eyes no longer felt useful, and my mind recaptured the moments of the battle from multiple angles in real time.

It was incredible and awful all at once. We followed the battle as it stormed through city block after city block, like watching a movie directed by Dr. Doom. Yet the awesome horror that came with knowing that what we were really doing, experiencing the chaos of a battle from many innocent bystanders' perspectives, was crippling. My lip quivered with the pain and anguish I felt knowing I was no different than the monsters we were watching.

"It takes time to get used to it," Samytus said after reading my face. "Imagine how I feel."

"Aren't you going to stop it?"

"I already have." He motioned with his hand in the direction of the battle, still partially visible through our new perspective.

Samytus's view showed that it was a mob of normals. Pissed normals. Some armed, some not, but all ready to die. Then the bloodshed began.

Courageous, abnormally fast, and often dead, the normals fell by the hundreds, but kept coming until the heroes in the battle were killed with their own weapons.

"They are like you, Roman Salt. They just remember how to fight."

Samytus cleared the window of his view, and it returned to the dusk setting it was before. Confused, hurt, and close to numb, I still couldn't help but to admire the city, even in its partial destruction. It was exactly what I had hoped the future would look like.

"The Employers told us this only ends with one of us standing," Samytus said while turning to face me. "I believe that to be true. The only problem is I don't think they were being clear. They wanted those like you to find and hunt those like me, and like your friend Drake."

"What do you mean?"

"The difference between you and those that tore those heroes apart just now is that the Employers randomly selected you. The difference between you and Drake is the same as between me and you."

"I still don't get what you're saying."

"Most of that isn't your fault. You weren't designed to. Just like the view you just experienced, you were lucky enough to be involved, instead of being a witness."

"So what am I?"

"Human."

"What are you and Drake?"

"Evolved."

"Fuck you."

"Thought you'd be happy to know your fate wasn't that of a hero—to be a god to some, but a monster to most."

"Why doesn't Drake know?"

"Who says he doesn't?"

"Again, fuck you."

"C'mon, Salt. Think about what I am saying. If the Employers want all like me hunted down and killed, and Drake is one of them, what incentive would he have in telling you?"

"He is far more powerful than me. He could've killed me long before now. I survived most of my closest brushes with death by…."

My thoughts knocked me cold with all the memories of our tall tale accomplishments. Never before did any of those memories feel corrupted. It was the only thing I had that the Employers didn't control. It was too much to think even for a second that all of it was altered by the only person I could call a friend.

Samytus didn't wait for me to recover. "I don't blame him, and I know you probably don't, either. My guess, he is doing like I am, and just trying to figure out a way out of this."

C H . 5 2
HEY, SOME KIDS
GET COAL IN
THEIR STOCKINGS

New Mexico, 2006

I went on to explain to Sunday that was how we got here. Samytus explained that he believed there were only three like him left: him, Drake, and the hero he sent us to kill in New Mexico. He felt that in doing so, the Employers would show their hand and allow him to strike at what he believed to be their source. At the very least, he thought the worst case scenario would be he finally exposed himself to the Employers he had been able to elude since the Battles began, and provide Drake and me the opportunity for the only salvation we would ever get—closure by being the one to kill the other. It really was all we could hope for.

"Do you believe him?" Sunday asked.

"Well, we were attacked by an Employer gunship on the way out of the city, but only after we cleared the fog that surrounds it."

"What about killing the hero he sent you and Drake here to kill? Why does he want Drake to kill him, and not you?"

"I thought you would know."

Sunday sprang up from the dead body. "Nope, kiddo. I lost you after you entered NLA."

"How'd you find me again?"

"I didn't know you were here until I shifted back from investigating who Samytus wanted dead next."

"What do you mean 'next'?"

"Haven't been keeping up, have you, sparky? Remember when I said Samytus was in league with the Employers? I wasn't lying. He's been hunting down heroes for a long time now, and he's hoping that he can force you into doing what the Employers can't."

"And what's that?"

"Erase this dimension. They can't control it, and all they have been trying to do since the Battles began is trying to systematically shut this dimension down by hunting the Relevant responsible for it. Samytus thinks that his power and his partnership with the Employers will keep his city safe. But he was always lazy with his power, and while focusing on creating realities for normals here, he didn't travel much.

"He hasn't seen what I have, and his powers blind him from the rest. The Employers aren't out to save anyone. They don't just shut down pesky dimensions—they are looking to eradicate all existence by hunting down every Relevant in the Realm."

"You're saying that we are existing in some hero's imagination?"

"I'm saying this isn't the dimension you were born in. This isn't your home."

Sunday paused to let what she was saying sink in. It was in that moment I understood why we had the conversation we just had, and why she needed to have it. She needed me to see before making her point.

"Think about everything you've told me you and Drake have done. Think about all the things you yourself said you did. Now, look at me," she said as she grabbed me by the front of my shirt. "Think about everything I've said. Heroes can only do what they do in someone else's dimension."

When Sunday was done looking at me and let go, my knees gave way. I collapsed back to the wall. Every memory I thought I buried of everyone I ever cared about erupted inside me. I felt everything, and then I felt nothing. And then I felt true fear for the first time, because I knew without a doubt I was alone.

"Do they exist? Did they?" I pushed out through a broken whisper.

"Who?"

"My family? My friends? Anyone I knew?"

I was asking her, but at that point in the life I had since the Battles, I failed to remember anyone. I remembered the idea of mourning them, or feeling the need to rectify the loss of their life and love. But now, with new perspectives, all I could remember was being alone.

"Not for me to say," Sunday replied.

"Then why should I care if existence ceases to exist or not?"

The music returned to regular speed. That's when I noticed I had left the faucet running. When I reached down to turn it off, Sunday was gone.

C H . 5 3
BEWARE THE BIGOTRY OF LOW EXPECTATIONS

I walked out to find Drake face-to-face with the stripper that was on stage when I went into the bathroom, and the bouncer that already wasn't a fan of us. A sentiment gained from the bouncer saying "Oh, these fucking guys…" under his breath as he let us in a few minutes ago.

It appeared that Drake had not held up his end of a bargain gone wrong. I wasn't completely sure what it was, but I was more engulfed his inexplicably nonviolent reaction to the situation.

Choosing to not let the luck of the uncommon lack of aggression in Drake turn, I grabbed him, apologized for whatever was the problem, and pushed him outside.

"I tell you, Salt, she had it coming," Drake half-heartily pleaded once we got outside.

"I'm sure she did, big guy."

"And where the fuck were you? Things could've gotten ugly in there. I called for you like…." Drake trailed off while he mentally tallied the times he actually called for me. "Well, I thought you'd be right back. What the hell were you doing?"

I thought about it for a moment. Something in me felt like it wasn't the time to tell him I was engaged in an hours-long conversation with a person that may have been a figment of my imagination.

"Brushing my teeth?"

"With what?"

"Funny enough, there was a toothbrush and toothpaste in there."

"And you just decided to use a random toothbrush?"

"When was the last time you brushed your teeth?"

Drake gave it some thought, then replied, "Tennessee."

"The battle at that indoor jungle hotel?"

"Yeah."

"One, when did you get time to do that? And two, that was months ago."

"Remember right before the Alt showed up and you were surrounded?"

"You son of a bitch."

"You had it."

"I almost didn't."

"But you did," Drake affirmed with a boisterous slap to the shoulder and finger gun gesture. "Doesn't matter. Still better than some random strip club toothbrush. That wasn't even in the dressing room, where you can assume it's at least coming from one of those clean ladies. You were in the public bathroom, where the wino vagrants come in to shit. I'm beginning to worry about your decision-making. No more drugs for you."

Beyond the insults and the fake embargo, the one thing that had been constant since this whole thing started was that Drake had been the only thing looking out for me. He cared for me, even if he struggled to understand how to show it.

But knowing all this did nothing in the face of the conversation with Sunday. She had no reason to lie. Would something as simple as emotion be the reason Drake would? Regardless of Sunday's intent, the seed of doubt of what Drake ultimately wanted was planted, cultivated with the question of why Lenny and Drake chose to partner with me. Before I could challenge that, a familiar voice with an unfamiliar accent interrupted.

"I know where you can find the hero Samytus sent you here to kill."

Drake and I turned to find Moses420 standing proudly before us. We didn't actually see him die, but it wasn't looking good for him. Yet here he was with a shit-eating grin. However, his accent belonged to a Middle Eastern man.

"How the fuck are you still alive?" Drake nodded toward Moses420.

"Funniest thing. Last thing I remember, I was holed up in some adobe, running out of ammo as the Alt closed in. Then the next moment, I'm in our boss's chamber."

"Boss? I think you got us confused, fucktard. We don't have bosses," Drake defied. "And where the fuck did that accent come from?"

"Why are you here?" Moses countered.

"Boredom."

"Where did Samytus send you?" I asked.

Ignoring the banter forming around whether or not Drake even had the same conversation with Samytus to make sense of what Moses meant, I felt like the conversation with Sunday was already morphing my sense of perception and what another hero meant, even when they weren't saying it out loud. I didn't need to know how Moses changed his accent so dramatically since the last time we met. That was obvious from knowing how long a hero could exist when shifted into other dimensions.

Now, I needed to know why they were sent to those dimensions at all. The clarity of his accent made it painfully clear that my quest for revenge on the Employers was going to be far from just killing what was in front of me.

My question drew a look of surprise on Moses. He knew its direction could only come from knowing what was possible in the reality we existed in.

"Many, many lives, my friend," Moses answered. "His vision is quite vast."

"The fuck are you ladies talking about?" Drake cut in.

"How do you know what Samytus wants from us?" I asked.

Not missing a beat over my perception change, Moses gave me a nod of acknowledgement and chose to skip the rest of the background formalities.

"As I said, boys, Samytus has vision. He knew she would try to find you and cloud your mind. She is quite good at it. Hell, I even saw Samytus use that skill to topple an entire civilization once. But she is lying to you."

"You don't know what she said to me, if anything at all."

"The fuck...? Salt, what is he talking about?"

Engaging with Drake and trying to explain to him what actually happened to me in the bathroom would be useless at this point. My best bet was to get as much from Moses before this conversation inevitably went south.

"You don't even know if she came to me at all. Matter of fact, who is this 'she' you are referring to?" I challenged.

Moses smiled at my choice to not acknowledge what he already knew, but his smile held nothing but misfortune. "Sure. Did you kill Serrick, then?"

"Haven't seen that guy since NLA."

"Perhaps he was killed by karma for tipping a stripper too lightly. Strange, I didn't see any heroes when I went in there after the two of you left."

"The bouncer was pretty tough. He looked like he could do some damage."

"Not battlebrace damage," Moses countered with a wink. "Even though that was my ride back, it doesn't matter to me. I never liked him. I'm sure Samytus can retrieve me when he wants me—like he did during that little standoff you two last saw me in. Until then, I think I'll just settle in around here. I think one of those strippers in there was sweet on me. As for you two, Samytus sent me here to make sure you go through with his request. Seeing that you lost your target after the crash, I figured I'd step in and guide you towards the right direction. Your hero is north of here, holed up in a little chapel on a hill."

"You've been spying on us?" Drake asked, as if that were the only thing he heard in everything Moses just said.

Before I, or Moses, could say a word, Drake impaled Moses and dropped him where he stood. Turning to me afterward, as if we both came to the same conclusion, he nonchalantly said, "Guess we go north."

C H . 5 4
PROMISED NOTHING

"So, you didn't think there wasn't any more to be gained from talking to a hero that somehow survived an Alt onslaught?" I asked while Drake and I proceeded to walk out of town.

I wasn't really sure why we both felt the need to walk to the destination Moses spoke of. The more I thought about it, the more it frightened me to remember that Moses never once mentioned where "north of here" meant. We were in New Mexico. North of there could literally mean sixteen states from here. Still, there was something in us both that felt like walking was the only option.

"Salt, he had the drop on us. You wanted him to have another shot?"

"Wasn't really worried about being able to take him. More the point about the same hero who sent a normal to get us just showed up and grabbed him out of the same situation we were in."

"You believe anything that fuck said?"

"We are walking north."

"Why the fuck not? We have nothing to do but find the next battle."

"But why are we walking?"

"I don't know. I just feel like it's close. Besides, we survived the same onslaught."

"We had to fucking work for it."

"Did we?"

It was at that point I realized we were far from the little town we just set off from not so long ago, or so I thought. Ahead of us was a lonely, old, decrepit chapel on a hill, miles off the road.

"What were you and Lenny talking about before you two approached me?"

Instead of surprising Drake, he seemed to have been expecting that question for quite some time.

"Whether we should kill you then and there."

In the same way Drake wasn't surprised by my question, I wasn't hurt by his response. Part of me couldn't let go how out of place I felt in all this. Sunday could have been wrong a thousand ways, but each way included a thousand versions of me. There only seemed to be one Lenny, one Drake, one Samytus, and one Sunday.

"Not sure, really. It was Lenny's idea. He said you didn't fit."

"And you?" I asked.

Drake swallowed his words and gave it a good meander until we were about a mile away from the chapel. The silly feeling that it took hours to walk the mile or so to the chapel from the road, but only seconds from the town to the road, challenged my concentration on Drake's refusal to answer. What did any of us have to lose?

"Because he needed you," said Mr. Polite, appearing through the chapel's entrance.

Alone and proud, he marched halfway toward us, then waited with his arms at his side, as if he were in service of us.

"Congratulations, Mr. Salt, Mr. Drake. You are the last two left. A battle between the two of you will end this all, and return peace to Earth. You should be quite—"

Something in me felt the deepest sense of jubilation, wicked or not, damned or not, after placing my sidearm to Mr. Polite's head and pulling the trigger. And although his head didn't explode as I fantasized myself to sleep many a night, it was still everything I'd hoped when I saw his lifeless body hit the ground.

Maybe it was because I feared what he was going to say next. Maybe I felt it was my only chance for any measure of personal revenge—even if avenging memories that don't belong to me. But most likely, I just didn't care anymore.

They were all gone. Taken from me and never coming back. There was no justice for that. Killing Polite was for pleasure. No sense in denying that.

C H . 5 5
SOMETHING   I
AM   MISSING

Once we crossed the threshold of the chapel, the last thing I remembered was the sound of a sidearm going off and a hot white flash. When I came to, I was sitting before a militaristic panel of seven. They sat in the shadows, on a makeshift platform crudely wedged into an office space not meant for staged platforms.

They were in the middle of talking, and after looking around a few times, it was clear they were addressing me. There was no one around me. No one guarding. I wasn't even bound. Just complacent in my surroundings.

Grumble this, grumble that, I really didn't care what they had to say until one of them pointed at me and hollered, "Whose hero will you become?"

When he said that, I was back in the white pulsating cell from before the Battles. The walls were pulsating in rhythm with my heart again, but this time, each pulse grew brighter and brighter. Just as the light became blinding, everything went dark, and I was left alone with my thoughts.

Only seconds had gone by, and all I could think was that it was the most silence I had experienced in longer than I could remember. I could hear myself for the first time. My breath, my heart, my thoughts—all there in brutal clarity.

The walls lit back up, but now each surface, including the ceiling, displayed cinematic replays of all the battles I had gone through. I watched, not with horror, but with an odd sense of pride at my growth throughout. I should have been ashamed at all the death that lay at my fingertips, with all the carnage playing out before me, but there was nothing in me to desire shame. There was no room.

My cinema of violence focused in on battles I was unaware of. I watched Drake and I cross the same desert landscape between the little town and the chapel, but this time, we weren't just talking.

We mowed through legions of the Alt, creating a sea of the dead, and didn't stop until we were at the base of the chapel's hill. That was when Polite showed up in the doorway. However, despite some pleading from Drake I didn't remember happening, I didn't give Polite time to address us. Nor did I care to watch him fall as I walked right past him, before his body even hit the ground.

The view focused in on the chapel, and I could no longer see Drake or myself, but some time went by. The setting around the chapel changed from day to night to dawn before anything else happened. Sandstorms began to form on the horizon and grew larger by the second, as if they were closing in on us.

I watched my body race toward a different village, further north of the chapel. When I got close, all I saw was pure rage. I ripped through a group of Alt entering a structure, following those I didn't kill into the building. The view on the walls lost sight of me, but I could see Drake sniping any and all that came after me.

The view quickly focused in on me leaping out of the top floor of the structure I just entered into the second floor of the building across from it. Meanwhile, Drake kept on taking out all the other Alt with fantastic precision.

Coming out of the building's entrance, I was met with a full detachment of Alt. Without hesitation, without regard for self, I charged at them as if they weren't there. I saw my body dance between them, alternating battleshotgun blasts with lethal slashes of the battlebrace. Those I didn't kill were brought down by Drake from distances unknown. We were death.

Before I could kill them all, the rest scurried away as one of the sandstorms got closer to us. Even in replay, I could hear and feel Drake pleading me to have caution. Instead, I saw myself disappear into the storm.

The view was nothing but the sandstorm now. It was beautifully chaotic. Sand, debris, and the occasional explosion or lightning strike—it looked as though the storm had captured destruction itself. And then the view panned up, where the sky was still clear and serene. Peaceful, even. And then that's when you see me falling from it.

Not out of control, not in complete, understandable fear, but with a battlebrace in the form of a sword ten times the size of my body. Right before I disappeared into the storm once more, I saw myself bring the blade forward, and watching from the cell, I could feel the energy of that level of rage again.

I wanted more.

C H . 5 6
C A M E L O T
DESERVED TO FALL

After a shudder and shake of the room, I was back in front of the panel. They continued to lecture and condemn me.

"Monster!" one shouted.

"Abomination," another condemned.

"Hero?" the middle one questioned. "You are no hero. But you can become one. Tell us!"

I felt more shuddering, but it wasn't from their condemnation. Everything shook. When it did, the judging panel made up of unknown military leaders flickered, and between each flicker, I saw white walls.

The last shudder brought dirt and pieces of the ceiling crashing down to the floor. Whatever was happening was happening to kill either me or them. The problem was the military panel continued to flicker, as if they weren't even there. Just me sitting alone, staring at a wall, insane and waiting for something to change. So insane, in fact, in the last flicker, I could've sworn I saw a hooded woman.

I've missed you.

Her thoughts invaded my mind. There was nothing I could do to stop it. We were connected in the most spiritual sense. It

was frightening and exhilarating at the same time, with such syn-
ergy between her mind and mine it was impossible to ignore the
notion that one came from the other, regardless of order.

That thought brought me back again to white cell I was in
before the Battles. Before, it was just a voice and my pulse; but
now, the voice had a persona—the hooded woman.

"Are you the Employers?"

The Employers don't exist.

"Then what is this? What have I've been doing all this time?
Where am I?"

Home.

"What is that? I don't understand. What is this place?"

Where you belong.

Anger and frustration coursed through my body, like a bad
shot of real shitty liquor after a long night of drinking. Everything in me wanted to fly out of my seat and wrap my hands
around her neck, but I couldn't.

Physically, I felt capable. I knew I could stand if I wanted to.
I looked down at my right hand, turning side to side as I gave it
the mental command. It was just that the one thing I wanted to
do was forbidden to my body.

"Why do I belong here?" I asked, understanding killing the
problem wasn't going to be the answer at present.

Because we made you.

"I think that was my parents' job."

You did not exist before us. What you remember is a lie.

"Fuck you. I don't believe you."

The woman forced visions and memories in my head. They
were so strong and complete but I felt down to my every fiber
they didn't belong to me. But they replayed in my head with clarity greater than those of my own family. The first vision was of me
of standing with some Alt on a building rooftop. We were looking down, waiting for something. A few more moments passed
by with idle talk of common history of survived battles against
godlike figures, until a group of lanky teens try to run through

the courtyard below. The vision ended with us lighting them up.

You killed them all for me.

My next vision brought me to the inside of a craft I could only assume belonged to the Employers. Once again, I was with the Alt, both sitting around and across from me. We were mentally preparing—getting ready for a fight. I could see some of them slightly nodding to themselves, while others checked the equipment of their squad mates to their left and right without prompting.

Just past the Alt sitting in front of me, I could see another transport racing alongside of us. We were flying at incredible speeds. The scenery around us became nothing more than streams of southwestern night schemes painted on a wall. The next second, everything dramatically slowed to a crawl but the screaming vibrant bolts of light that began to flash between me and the other transport.

The other transport ignited with incredible light, illuminating everything with terrifying clarity. I saw every one of them. One made eye contact with me and placed his hand on the window he was looking out, before he and the rest of the transport violently crumpled away out of sight. Speed returned to my memory, and left it with our transport barrel-rolling out of enemy fire with one of the Alts standing in front of the cockpit, barking orders.

I have always been with you.

Suddenly, I was in a nondescript urban suburb of the kind littered throughout the country. I was walking toward two Alts talking to a normal. The notion of the Alt actually communicating with people was odd, but not more than the feeling of comfort I had walking with the other Alt as we approached the group.

A woman approached the group before we reached them. She wore a full body suit, as the Alt did, but white. Her head was only covered in a hood fitted tight to her head, but stiffly hung out at an angle that left everything in shadows except for her glowing red lips.

She directed the conversation with an air of supremacy that it made it clear challenging her would bring something greater than death. Before we could reach them to hear what was being said, an explosion blew open the top floor of the building we were standing in front of.

A hero jumped out and immediately began firing at the sky. At first, it looked like he was delirious. But then, several other heroes acrobatically leapt from the rooftop in pursuit. All the Alt around me took off toward the battle, running past the woman, who was in the process of executing the normal she was speaking to while looking directly at me.

Too paralyzed by the threat of any of this being true, I didn't have enough energy to protest. Instead, I just felt it, until it verbalized internally.

I don't believe you, I thought back.

Again, my beautiful weapon, you don't have to.

Her hands didn't move—or at least, I didn't see them move—but her thoughts caressed me underneath my chin, as a mother would her child. I hated that I found comfort in it. I could feel her need to ease my pain.

No. None of that happened. I don't remember any of that, I continued to protest.

You don't remember much from the last several Earth years.

It's only 2007, I returned, doing my best to hide the defeat in my thoughts.

It hasn't been 2007 for quite some time.

I became overwhelmed with emotion as a wave of memories and experiences washed over me. Things I didn't even know existed found space in previously ignored recollections as if they have always been there—far more experiences that one could gain in a single lifetime.

What do you want from me? I asked, finally broken.

Stay with me.

Ch. 57
Executioner Style

Her last thought brought me back to the mysterious military tribunal/kabuki theater in a dentist's office. Two of the giant bald freaks always with Polite burst through the side door. It didn't matter if the panel had more condemnation for me, whatever this was was over—and with little protest.

The Hosts themselves were different. Gone were the impeccably fitted suits. Now, they had donned tactical gear underneath obscurely wrapped dark tunics.

They dragged me down the hall. After a few feet, I found myself more amazed that they created a base of operations in what was definitely a family dental practice than I was focused on where they were taking me. In each room we passed, I saw the Hosts moving in diligent silence. They were preparing for something.

We passed an intersection where I could see that the main base of operations was in the practice's general waiting area. Multiple screens were set up on the receptionist's desk with one Host manning the feeds while several others hovered over him. They were trying to locate something, and cared little about the other Hosts frantically preparing around them.

The building shook once more. This one was enough to knock the Hosts dragging me a little off-balance and shake the feeds on the monitors.

Every screen went to static, then came back on one by one. Before being dragged too far to see anything else, I could see some of the feeds catch an Alt walking casually down a hallway. It wasn't until he was almost at the floor's next hallway intersection that I realized he was coming down the corridor intersecting ours.

The Alt got to the intersection and tucked his head, as if he was trying his hardest to locate something on the ground without bending down to get a closer look. Instead of continuing forward, the Hosts dropped me and charged toward the Alt. Watching the monitors, I saw multiple Hosts doing the same from all four directions.

The first Host met the Alt's fist as the tall and lean figure delivered a blow so powerful it doubled over the massive beast. Everything else was a blur, save the last moment before the Alt extended his battlebrace through the Host, then stealthily retracted it as if the strike were meant to be a secret.

The Alt shifted under one attack, only to wrap around the attacker to kick the next one in the head. He then shifted under the powerful swing of the Host attacking him from behind, only to emerge around the other side and kill the unsuspecting Host behind the attacker.

The Alt found himself in the middle of the Hosts again. Waiting until the most aggressive threw a punch, he caught it and held it while he used that to propel defensive attacks on all the Hosts closing in on him. When that ran its course, the Alt somersaulted over the Host, with the giant's fist and arm still in a vicelike grip, then let go to kick him forward into the Host standing in front of him.

Turning underneath a near fatal strike from the Host coming behind him, the Alt launched a machinegun assault with his fists, pausing only to backhand the Host from the side and deflect an attack. He came back around to deliver a brutal upward swing with his battlebrace to decapitate the Host still recovering from the punches.

The last Host stood between me and the Alt, now calmly approaching. The comfort and ease in his stride, in contrast to the retreating Host, was profound. No battlebrace activated, no weapon in hand, this Alt intended on killing the Host with fear alone.

The Host probably meant to attack the approaching Alt, but the directness of the Alt paralyzed him. The Alt, in one fluid motion, grabbed the Host's head and ran along the hallway walls for a full revolution, then swung down to the Host's side and let go. The Alt had his hand out for me to take before the dead Host hit the ground.

C H . 5 8
ALWAYS   THERE

I spat at the hand and got up to push him away. I was hoping to impale him with a battlebrace—or two—but that was when I noticed they were no longer attached to my arms.

With nothing to fight with, and the strong assumption my activeskin was gone as well, I took off down the hallway the Alt appeared from. Strangely enough, when I took off for the door, it looked like it was only fifty feet away or so. But my mind tore at that notion when I finally reached it several minutes later.

The door didn't lead to outside, but to a series of tunnels that felt like they were descending underground. Either Dr. Blatt's fine dentistry was also the front to a Batcave, or the Employers had set up operations here some time ago.

And then it hit me. If that were the case, then what was I running from, and to where? Better still, why did an Alt have to save me from an Employer operation? And then I begin to lose it.

My brain froze in agony, as if I were challenging a worse brain freeze than eating a hundred Icees in a row. Each section felt like it was at war with another. The frontal lobe was in conflict with the cortex. The left and right battled like the Civil War. Nothing felt safe.

Every thought betrayed me. Every notion of believing I belonged to people, that I had a family and friends—all felt engineered. Every memory of the stranger that became my brother, Drake, felt toxic.

Begging for death was an afterthought. That still had the tacit promise of an afterlife. I wanted nothing more with existence. I began to feel like a mistake of unparalleled portions, an aberration of existence.

Despite hearing the sounds of the ocean, I ran into what I believed to be a dead end, until the Alt I was running from casually walked past me and through the wall. Seeing that I had no choice, I followed him through the wall, only to walk into a massive hanger bay on the other end. It was similar to the cloud station Lenny brought us to, except this one had a very much still-fucking-alive Mr. Polite waiting for me.

"Fuck me. And just when I thought I was getting good at something. Well, if you aren't dead, then at least tell me I am."

"Would that be preferable?"

"Yes."

"Where do you think you are?"

"I don't know."

"When do you think it is?"

"I haven't a clue."

"Who do you think you are?"

I started to answer that question, but stumbled at the notion of the answer. The further away from the beginning of the Battles, the less I remembered anything about me, save my name.

"Walk with me," Polite offered.

We walked down the hangar, toward what seemed to be the bay's exit, but all I saw was blackness. Polite didn't speak again until we came to the giant doors. As we approached within several feet, they slid open, exposing us to the glorious sight of the sun triumphantly shimmering over a never-ending ocean horizon.

C H . 5 9
R E M E M B E R
THE   ZOMBIES!

"Beautiful, isn't it? We have travelled many worlds, many dimensions, but few grander in sight than this one. I see now why she chose this place. She hates beauty. It reminds her of home."

"Who? The hooded woman in the white cell?"

Polite scoffed, and laughed off such a suggestion as if the thought of even entertaining it was offensive. "A funny thing, relationships. In some places, the very idea doesn't exist. Futile attempts to avoid the inevitable, if you ask me. Relationships are in everything. Everything is connected. What do you think you are looking at?"

"The ocean," I answered plainly.

Polite held out his hand. It reached just beyond the hangar's edge. From there, he extended one finger and said, "What was California."

He pulled his hand back and looked at me. I wasn't too far gone to confuse his facial expression for anything close to empathy, or at least, sympathy. But there was a sense of discernment for my current plight.

"It is all over," Polite confirmed.

"NLA?"

"Gone, during the bombardment that resulted in the New Mexican ocean side property we found you in."

"Why find me? Didn't you already have me?"

"Who do you think had you?"

"The Employers. There were Hosts all over the place. Some shadowy military suits talking about me letting them down, and then the white cell with the hooded woman. Same as before. Same as when I first saw you in the Common."

Polite now held out both his hands and put them in front of him. Once his hands were together, he separated them like theater curtains and said, "Allow me to paint you a different picture than the vibrant one you covet so vividly in your thoughts.

"Imagine if the battles you fought weren't battles, but extinction-level multidimensional war sagas personified in single beings. If you accept any of that premise, then you must accept that those beings are capable of limitless possibilities. Surely something that can conjure up a dimension could perform many other feats. What if one feat was to develop other beings not like them to fight for them, or simply to use as a weapon in their current conflict? I'm sure you can think of when maybe a soldier would eschew reloading his or her weapon and improvise with whatever is around them?"

Polite said as he began to circle around me. "Perhaps you have done so as well?"

"What are you saying?" I asked, nearly pleading.

I had little ability left to mentally leap around the pitfalls in trying to understand someone, or something, that was vastly more knowledgeable in current events than I. Even if Polite was filled with lies, what he said had more substance than the thoughts I'd been trying to not entertain since the strip club. Namely, the thought of not actually existing. The thought of knowing that even if there were an afterlife, it wasn't for me. Part of me felt weird that in most ways, I was okay with that. If anything Sunday said was right, then I didn't deserve an afterlife. But all of me did everything possible to avoid thinking there wasn't an afterlife for those I loved and lost.

"You remember the Common because that is when your time on this planet began."

"No."

"One of your friends brought you here to fight for them. We aren't sure which one. We lost track of their souls when their false versions on this planet were killed."

Every part of me sunk into itself. The emptiness I felt would challenge any abyss. I fought hard, harder than any battle I survived, to think of my family. The harder I tried, the more vague they became.

"No. No! I fucking exist, goddamn it!" I shouted.

"No doubt you did, just not here. This planet is a replica, created by one of the beings I speak of. This was what all this was for, the Battles—to find the source of this replicated planet. What you call "the Employers" is really the Vangard, the military banner of a species known as the Seraph. Their single charge is to eliminate all life beneath their dimension. What you think you were forced to do was really a hunt on their behalf, while they sat back and cherry picked beings that showed great potential."

"You were there. I saw you."

"In the Common? No, what you witnessed was one of your friends running a mock version of what you believe the start of the Battles was. The Battles began about a year before you think."

"You lost me."

"Do you remember zombies?"

C H . 6 0
Empathy Won't Save Those in the Path of a Landslide

Everything—and I do mean everything—I thought I knew was wrong. Everything. My life didn't belong to me.

I wanted to believe he was wrong. I wanted to believe Polite was telling me what I feared the most only to break me. But it was becoming clear that whatever my new fate would be, what I wanted wouldn't mean a hill of shit in the path of a landslide hoping to be stopped or slowed with slight elevation.

Polite continued to paint his version of my past. The white cell was an actual location found somewhere within the Vangard. But more than just being a room, it was a device the Seraph used to recreate a "life" for the abducted. Once the Seraph felt the process was complete, they would release the abducted back into the environment and force them hunt one another.

Polite believed that was because part of the process was replicating a mental connection the Scions, those I called "the Alt," and their military banner, the Cross, utilized. Because it was as much a trial and error process as the hunt for Relevants and Recluses, some of the abducted took longer than others to take, as evident with the zombies in the Common. This was also the case when a Relevant or Recluse recklessly ripped beings from other dimensions to fight and die for them during a battle.

I was one of the zombies. I stood there in the Common, aimless and soulless, along with the rest of the lost souls that called the Common their home. Most likely written off as a homeless junkie, people probably didn't bat an eye when they saw me, or any like me, out there in the dead of winter to the unforgiving heat of the summer, looking unfazed by any of it.

And this was where my incredible fight for life and survival came to an end, as well as the crash landing of the notion of having a soul. Those from dimensions belonging to a Relevant or Recluse, as opposed to those of the original dimensions of the Realm, couldn't connect to the Vangard without the white cell. Aside from my inane rants of self and fate, the only other sound in my head through the Battles was the screams of those I killed.

Hell, there were some nights I prayed for a new voice to fill my head. But no, only the true souls of original dimensions made a distant connection to the Vangard, as the Scions can with the Cross. The rest of us were nothing more than residual existences born out of imagination, and not of the substance that brought existence to the souls of the original dimensions, to the Vangard and the Cross, and to the gods we here on Earth thought we prayed to.

"Whether learned or innate, you mourn the dead. That is a good sign," Polite tried to console.

"Does it mean I ever had a family?"

"There is no way of telling that. The fact that you are still existing now with those that are dead in this dimension says you at least have something to live for."

"What's that?"

"I am a Construct. I am an algorithm of thoughts, ideas, philosophies, and historical records. I exist only because of others. The only difference between you and I is that my makeup isn't based on DNA, but on all the elements I listed, spanning over the entirety of the Realm. You were born, most likely from two parents...." Polite paused to wave off my confusion. "It gets quite confusing in some dimensions. Believe me.

"Your parents had parents, and so on and so forth. It just wasn't here, and it is nearly a certainty that it wasn't from a planet of the original dimensions. Most have been wiped out by now."

"Then why was I here?"

"We have strong reason to believe it was the Relevant the Vangard came here to hunt. We are struggling to confirm that, because you killed all of our leading prospects. We also believe that is why the Seraph are done hunting, and have moved onto bombarding this planet until there is nowhere for the Relevant to hide. They'll either find it, or leave the planet devoid of life and post a sentry here to report when anything changes."

"Drake?"

"Not, him, and not Lenny. Not even Sunday, who was the target of Vangard all along."

"Why not them?"

"We lost contact with our forces in all the dimensions belonging to your friend Lenny. The same for the Vangard. For that to happen, the source had to have been killed. We found Lenny's body out in the desert, amongst the debris of a Vangard cloud station."

"Sunday said he wasn't from here."

"A thousand lies..." Polite teased, reminding me that my thoughts of what happened in the past were well known to him. "The Vangard chooses to force suspected Relevants and Recluses into situations like the Battles, because the life belonging to the Relevant or Recluse can't help but to fight. Most find it by accident, some find it by emotion, but the Battles find all.

"Lenny was strong, and far more advanced than even some of the original dimension Relevants and Recluses. But he was only as strong as the being responsible for this planet. When he died here, there was no escape for his soul but to go back to whomever or whatever it belonged to—meaning his version here was the original that belonged to the Relevant the Vangard are hunting down."

"Drake?" I repeated.

Polite could see Drake was all I had left. There was no guarantee if what I believed to be memories of my life before the Battles held any authenticity, but my time with Drake did. He became my brother, and maybe the only family I ever had.

"Drake," I demanded.

"You killed him," Polite answered.

Numbness set in like a virus and wormed its way to my core, shutting everything down in the process. I had nothing left.

In some ways, I wanted to hear what Polite had to say next. But that desire paled in comparison to wanting to kill whatever he was at that moment. Even for the sake of my pseudo-sanity I couldn't take hearing what he had to say next.

My hands wrapped around his neck. For a "Construct," it felt every bit like grabbing the neck of the living. In the same moment we locked eyes, my arms tightened and I flung him over the ledge.

Tears rushed down my face as fell to my knees, heaving with air. I couldn't get enough. The more I inhaled, the more I drowned in the flooding tears. I had nothing left. With my rage abated, nothing more.

Exist or not, every part of me wanted to live. Almost my way of saying "Fuck you" to the circumstance that created me. As if it were my last action, I found all the remaining strength left in my body and got myself off the ground. Turning around to leave, I was greeted by a sea of Scions, and the very soul I just threw over the edge.

EPILOGUE
YOU MAY FIND
RDEMPTION
IN THE CHAOS

Grand Canyon, 2190

After days of tracking, a lone Scion came upon his target, camouflaged among the stalactites hanging down from the cavern ceiling.

"You can come on down, Seraph. Let's end this."

Nothing moved. Patiently, the Scion continued to talk. "No sense in keeping this up. Rocks don't have glowing eyes."

Checking over his gear while waiting for the large being to come down and face him, he didn't even notice the search had moved into its sixth morning until the rising sun behind him splashed light into the cavern, stopping in between him and his target. He also didn't care.

The winged being detached from its hiding spot and fell to the ground before the Scion. Landing on one knee, the being was already twice his height. It towered over the Scion when it finally rose on two feet. Its wings swiftly wrapped tightly around its body, producing a multi-robed uniform in the process.

"Scion."

"Seraph."

"The lone hero, come to kill the last of the monsters, is it?"

"I'm not alone, and you aren't the last."

The Seraph's face wrinkled into an amused grimace. His glowing eyes contrasted the darkness of his side of the cavern, creating sinister shadows to his smile.

"You are alone. All of you. Why do you think you where the suit?"

"Am I to believe a Seraph had me track him all the way out here for a history in fashion? Come on. Die like the high-dimensional being you claim to be, and let's be done with it."

"You've killed a lot of Seraphs—the Vangard has no doubt in that. You seem to like it."

"I do."

"And rightfully so. To some, our motives may seem cruel, but that is to be expected amongst the pests. But tell me—in the life you remember before, did you stop to explain your actions before killing the thing infesting your world? I think not. However, in time, all will be corrected, and existence will begin anew, this time properly."

"Part of the reason I enjoy it is that sentiment right there."

"Hmph. The Cross is no different. You slice through legions of us as if we don't exist, but fail to realize the one responsible for your fate fights alongside you."

"Enough. Let's be done with this, Seraph."

The Seraph let out a peal of thunderous laughter, as well as his massive wings—exposing his monstrously strong physique. "That is why I am telling you. You still think he is dead."

The Seraph swung his right wing down in a powerful arc. It barely swept past the dodging Scion and ripped through the cavern wall. A body-smashing fist drove into the ground right as the Scion moved past it and up the Seraph's exposed arm. Once at the Seraph's shoulders, the Scion created a chain with his battlebraces, and wrapped it around the Seraph's neck.

A burst of energy allowed the Seraph to rip the Scion from its back and heave him forward. After a few out of control tumbles, the Scion got to his feet. He continued to slide until he used his battlebraces to dig into the ground and slow his momentum.

"They told you he killed her?" the Seraph began.

"Who?" 143 yelled.

"Sunday and Drake. Did they tell you Drake killed Sunday?"

"All fucking lies. You clearly are ready to die, considering you chose to hide here instead of retreating home. You knew I would find you here. You know what I do. Hurry up and die, already!"

"'A thousand lies.' 'Whose hero will you become?' That all came from us! What you remember was from the white cell, including what the Cross told you before they actually broke you out."

"I was freed in New Mexico."

"Freed? Pff. You had to be taken before you were freed."

"So now I am to believe a Seraph that knows he is about to die?"

"You should. You've been a Scion of the Cross for millions of years. You were here to hunt both Sunday and Drake."

Flashbacks stormed 143's mind, crippling him in the process. His memory raced back to the moments before the chapel some hundreds of years ago. This time, unlike any time before, he saw it from a different view. He was back in the transport he envisioned the last time he was in the Vangard's white cell.

The transport barely made it to its drop point after surviving a surprise attack and losing part of the convoy. 143 and his detachment rushed out, along with dozens of other Scions landing at the same time.

They all fearlessly stormed the chapel, where one hero looking like Drake had just executed a hero resembling Sunday. When the Scions drew close, the surviving hero turned his attention toward them.

The hero threw a towering mech from out of the thin air at the charging Scions. The giant war machine launched a missile strike like a meteor shower on the Scions. Most perished, but a few danced on top of each explosion like powerful steps to evade.

The first Scion to reach the mech leapt out of sight, using parts of the mech in his ascent. The remaining Scions dodged the pounding attacks of the colossus that quickly moved on from the first Scion, who disappeared into the cloudy skies above.

Massive in stature, the mech lagged behind the deft Scions, but not by much. Right as it was beginning to interpret the Scions' attack and evasion patterns, the Scion that disappeared into the clouds returned with an energy blade from his combined battlebraces.

The Scion brought his sword down into the head of the mech and rode it down, cleaving it in half in the process. Once his feet met the ground, he and the remaining Scions continued on toward the hero without hesitation.

Unlike any other holding a BSR, the hero masterfully took out all but the Scion 143 connected to in the vision he was having. 143 watched the last Scion close the distance between himself and the hero. The Scion slid to the side of the hero's last-ditch attempt to hit him with the BSR. The hero jumped back just in time to miss the Scion's swing of a battlebrace to the midsection as the Scion cut the BSR in half with his other blade.

Using the momentum of the Scion's swing, the hero followed that up by grabbing the swinging arm and pulling it down, aided by a punch to the Scion's head. The Scion rode the last motion and fed into the pulling. He rolled around the hero to kick him in the face.

Recoiling back into the chapel, the hero chose that as a time to escape by jumping through the stained glass in the back. He tore off into the desert with the Scion on his heels.

The Scion caught the hero once more, causing the hero to stop. Down to only his sidearms, the hero wielded them like a sword and shield against a dragon. He used one to make the Scion change his direction, while the other went for the kill. Every shot was met with the Scion moving like he knew what was coming before the hero had a chance to do it.

The hero shot at the Scion's feet, only to have the Scion step next to where he fired. The hero then shot to the side in anticipation of the Scion's sidestep, but the Scion missed it by approaching directly. The Scion took a few hits of the hero's sidearm to get an advantage, then avoided the rest like a phantom.

Now close enough, the Scion waited until the hero went to shoot at him again, then embraced him with a battlebrace blade splitting through the hero's chest. The hero fought with all the life he had left to get another shot off, but the Scion held him too close for that. Breaking from the robotic approach the Cross had to take when taking a life, the Scion held the dying hero close, making sure the hero wouldn't feel like he was dying alone. The hero whispered into the ear of the Scion before falling to the ground.

The Scion's vision returned to the present.

"What is this?" he demanded from the Seraph.

"They lied to you. They told you you didn't exist, and that you killed him. They told you that you don't belong to him because you still exist after killing him. All lies. You and he existed at the same time. Still do. That is what he whispered to you, isn't it?"

"There was no whisper," 143 growled.

The Seraph laughed once more. "They already lied to you. How long were you supposed to be on Replica Earth? How long were any of us?"

"The Vangard abducted us."

"Over a hundred years, Scion," the Seraph answered his own question. "We only had you for three."

"No!"

"Seems we are all liars, Scion. You, me, the Cross. Except, unlike you, I am not just a soulless weapon." The Seraph sneered.

The Scion shot forward, deftly evading Seraph's retreating attacks. Before the Seraph could recover, the Scion was on the Seraph's chest. They both fell back as the Scion drove a battlebrace blade through the Seraph's sternum.

When the two landed, the Scion rolled off of the dying

Seraph as it fought for life through gurgling blood. Surprisingly, he laughed mightily, spewing Seraph blood all over like demonic sprinkler.

"You are older than you could imagine. You hate me because you were there during the fall, and you remember what we've done," the Seraph spat out. "But you forget—so were they."

His eyes and mouth let out a hiss, and then dullness set in before going completely black. The light intensified in his torso before emitting a brilliant, blinding glow for a few seconds. Then, the light eroded the body into dust.

The Scion returned to the canyon peak he had left nearly a week ago at the start of the hunt. There, waiting for him, was the Construct. Odd, considering it had been quite some time since the Construct met him out on the hunt.

"143," the Construct said as the Scion joined his side to peer out into the Canyon.

"Polite," 143 returned.

"Did you find what you were looking for?"

"I believe so."

"Did you find anything more?"

143 turned to look directly the Construct. "Should I have?"